"You're quite an actress, aren't you?"

"What in the world are you talking about?"

"All that sentimental garbage about your bad childhood. It was merely a ploy to gain my sympathy, wasn't it?"

Her face paled, and her shock looked genuine. "That is probably the vilest, lowest thing anybody has ever said to me. I'm sorry I ever confided in you. And even sorrier I ever met you."

Matt cornered her, and now she was on the run. He blocked her escape.

"If you don't step aside I'm going to…to…" Sandi sagged, the fight suddenly gone out of her. She covered her face with her hands and made a sound that nearly broke his heart. The heart he'd tried so hard to keep deep-frozen and safe.

"Sandi…" Her shoulders shook; her whole body shook. Alarmed, Matt touched her arm, and that was all it took.

Suddenly she was in his arms, her face pressed tightly against his chest, wetting the front of his tuxedo with her tears. He patted her shoulders, stroked her hair, smoothed her back.

Then magically everything changed. He was no longer comforting her, and s̲ sobbing. They were touchin in, giving up, giving over t̲ that arced between them…

Dear Reader,

Your best bet for coping with April showers is to run—not walk—to your favorite retail outlet and check out this month's lineup. We'd like to highlight popular author Laurie Paige and her new miniseries SEVEN DEVILS. Laurie writes, "On my way to a writers' conference in Denver, I spotted the Seven Devils Mountains. This had to be checked out! Sure enough, the rugged, fascinating land proved to be ideal for a bunch of orphans who'd been demanding that their stories be told." You won't want to miss *Showdown!*, the second book in the series, which is about a barmaid and a sheriff destined for love!

Gina Wilkins dazzles us with *Conflict of Interest,* the second book in THE McCLOUDS OF MISSISSIPPI series, which deals with the combustible chemistry between a beautiful literary agent and her ruggedly handsome and reclusive author. Can they have some fun without love taking over the relationship? Don't miss Marilyn Pappano's *The Trouble with Josh,* which features a breast cancer survivor who decides to take life by storm and make the most of everything—but she never counts on sexy cowboy Josh Rawlins coming into the mix.

In Peggy Webb's *The Mona Lucy,* a meddling but well-meaning mother attempts to play Cupid to her son and a beautiful artist who is painting her portrait. Karen Rose Smith brings us *Expecting the CEO's Baby,* an adorable tale about a mix-up at the fertility clinic and a marriage of convenience between two strangers. And in Lisette Belisle's *His Pretend Wife,* an accident throws an ex-con and an ex-debutante together, making them discover that rather than enemies, they just might be soul mates!

As you can see, we have a variety of stories for our readers, which explore the essentials—life, love and family. Stay tuned next month for six more top picks from Special Edition!

Sincerely,

Karen Taylor Richman
Senior Editor

Please address questions and book requests to:
Silhouette Reader Service
U.S.: 3010 Walden Ave., P.O. Box 1325, Buffalo, NY 14269
Canadian: P.O. Box 609, Fort Erie, Ont. L2A 5X3

The Mona Lucy

PEGGY WEBB

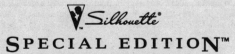

Silhouette®

SPECIAL EDITION™

Published by Silhouette Books

America's Publisher of Contemporary Romance

For Michael with love.

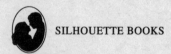 SILHOUETTE BOOKS

ISBN 0-373-24534-3

THE MONA LUCY

Copyright © 2003 by Peggy Webb

This edition published by arrangement with Harlequin Books S.A.

® and TM are trademarks of Harlequin Books S.A., used under license.
Trademarks indicated with ® are registered in the United States Patent
and Trademark Office, the Canadian Trade Marks Office and in other
countries.

Visit Silhouette at www.eHarlequin.com

Printed in U.S.A.

Books by Peggy Webb

PEGGY WEBB

and her two chocolate Labs live in a hundred-year-old house not far from the farm where she grew up. "A farm is a wonderful place for dreaming," she says. "I used to sit in the hayloft and dream of being a writer." Now, with two grown children and more than forty-five romance novels to her credit, the former English teacher confesses she's still a hopeless romantic and loves to create the happy endings her readers love so well.

When she isn't writing, she can be found at her piano playing blues and jazz, or in one of her gardens planting flowers. A believer in the idea that a person should never stand still, Peggy recently taught herself carpentry.

Dear Reader,

When I wrote *The Accidental Princess* I had no idea I was writing the first book in a series about THE FOXES—Sorority sisters grown up and long out of college—but I loved the characters so much that they stayed in my mind awaiting their turn on center stage. *The Mona Lucy* continues the story of these funny, passionate, tender characters in a book that is Southern from cover to cover.

The Mona Lucy brings back the hopeful romantic Sandi Wentworth, as well as the irrepressible O'Banyon and Coltrane women whose scheming sets the stage where love blossoms amongst merry mayhem.

I grew up and still live in rural Mississippi, and I have a deep, abiding love for small-town characters with all their eccentricities. A host of O'Banyons and Coltranes are still waiting in the wings to tell their stories. I hope you will laugh and cry with these characters, that you will root for them, love them and stay with them as I spin out their wonderful tales of romance.

Happy reading!

Peggy Webb

Chapter One

Matt Coltrane hadn't wanted to come to the wedding. Thank God it was almost over. The reception was winding down—mainly because everybody was getting drunk—and Matt could soon go home.

He didn't believe in love or matrimony. Marriage only led to divorce, as far as he was concerned. He ought to know; he'd handled enough of them in the past fourteen years to make a man think twice and then some before he took that suicidal walk down the aisle. Or in this case, around the corner of his mother's swimming pool, which was the only reason he was here.

Lucy O'Banyon Coltrane had offered her house and grounds for the wedding of her prim and proper college roommate and sorority sister, Ellie Jones, and she'd asked Matt to be there "in case somebody falls into the pool."

"That's a ridiculous reason for me to drive three hundred miles," he'd told his mother when she called. "Nobody's going to fall into the pool."

"Yes, but in case they do, you'll know how to handle it. And besides, I haven't seen you in weeks."

He'd driven up from Jackson, Mississippi, to Shady Grove out of guilt and had stayed out of curiosity. Members of the Foxes, the sorority his mother helped charter, had flown in from all over the country to celebrate the wedding of one of their own. One of them was the U.S. attorney general. Matt had hoped to talk with her, but she'd called at the last minute to cancel.

The entire event was over the top, if anybody had asked Matt's opinion, on the hottest day of June, all these candles adding to the heat. They knew better, of course. He was not the type of man to withhold his opinions. He was trying hard not to put a damper on the celebration.

God knows, he'd done nothing but scowl since he got there. You couldn't move without stepping over a bridesmaid. There was a flock of fifteen, wearing those ridiculous hats, no two alike, all dressed in pink.

It was a pure relief to spot a woman dressed in green. She was on the other side of the pool, her shoes kicked off, snapping pictures and attracting a crowd. Men, of course. So many swooning swains gathered around her that Matt had to stand up to see.

His mother slid into a chair at his table. "Lovely, isn't she?"

He nonchalantly eased into his chair. "Who?"

"The photographer. Don't think I didn't see you watching her. I think she's quite charming."

"Don't start," he said, and Lucy gave him a crest-fallen look. "All right. I concede. She's easily the most striking woman here."

"See, I told you you'd be glad you came."

"Now, Mother, get that look out of your eye. I came for you. That's all."

"I'm glad you did, Matt. Since you're here, why don't you go around the pool and introduce yourself to that delightful-looking woman."

Matt would rather eat arsenic. Women in general were dangerous, but women of her kind were lethal. They reeled you in with their innocent act then knifed you in the back. That angel's face didn't fool him. Inside that sweet little package beat the heart of a barracuda.

"She's not my type," he said.

"You shouldn't let one bad experience color your opinions."

One bad experience wouldn't begin to describe the events that had colored his opinions. But he would never tell anyone, least of all his mother.

"Can I get you some more food, Mother?"

Lucy got that same look she always got when she was all set to deliver a rare motherly lecture, but this time Matt stared her down. She sighed.

"No, thank you, dear. I'm on a diet."

"Why? You look fine to me."

"I don't want to look fine. I want to look *great*. Like Dolly."

"Where is Aunt Dolly?" She wasn't really his aunt, but he'd called her that for so long she might as well have been. Of all the Foxes, she was his favorite.

"Quaffing booze and flirting, no doubt."

"I'd better see if I can find her."

"She'll be mad as a hornet if you try to drag her away from one of her little peccadilloes, as she calls them."

"We'll see about that."

As Matt set out to rescue the indomitable actress Dolly Wilder from her baser impulses, a green hat lifted on the breeze, sailed across the pool and landed at water's edge practically at his feet.

He scooped the hat out of the water and strode around the pool to give it back to its owner.

The wind that had stolen her hat whipped her dress and her long blond hair. She was a beautiful woman, fresh-scrubbed and wholesome. Just like his ex-fiancée. A heartless floozy in disguise.

"My hat! You found it."

She turned her flutelike voice and innocent-looking green eyes on him, and Matt came within a hairbreadth of succumbing to her siren song. After all, he *was* human, in spite of rumors to the contrary.

The sooner he got out of there, the better. He rammed the hat into her hand, then watched in mortification as it dripped on the shoes she'd kicked off, leaving huge water spots.

Obviously her shoes were dyed-to-match silk, a fact

he wouldn't have known if he hadn't grown up in a household with two sisters.

Matt didn't know whether to kneel down and try to wipe her shoes dry or to let well enough alone.

"Sorry about the shoes," he said. His cohorts would die laughing if they could hear him. The man known in the courtroom as Bulldog Coltrane was acting like a nervous Chihuahua. His only saving grace was that he hadn't tried to put the soggy hat back on her head.

"Oh, it's no problem. I'm going to throw them away anyhow. They pinch my toes."

Matt didn't want to make small talk with this woman, but Lucy had tried to teach him to be a gentleman and he guessed some of her lessons stuck.

As he cast about for an escape tactic, he spotted the perfect one: Aunt Dolly sashaying to his mother's table looking none too steady on her spike-heeled shoes.

Before he could excuse himself, the woman said, "You're the strong silent type, aren't you?"

Good God. She was worse than Matt had thought. "No," he said. "Mainly I'm the surly type." Then he scowled at her just to prove it.

The woman was not the least bit discouraged. "Look at that terrific hat," she said.

Who could miss it? It stood out like an oversize hippo in the *Swan Lake* ballet. He watched as his aunt Kitty O'Banyon made a beeline for his mother's table, her hat bobbing with every step.

"I wish I had one like that. I wonder where she got it?"

"It came as a gift with the case of tequila she ordered from Mexico."

"You know her?"

"Yes." He didn't bother telling her the family relationship.

"Such a strong, arresting face. I'd love to paint her."

The next thing he knew, the woman would be wanting to meet Kitty, and since he wasn't a total cad he couldn't very well turn her down. Then before he could blink twice, his mother and Aunt Dolly and Aunt Kitty would have her booked for lemon-balm tea on Tuesdays and bad tennis on Wednesdays and arguments over Eastern religious philosophy every Saturday, and there would be no way in heaven or on earth Matt could avoid seeing her again.

He never would have rescued her hat in the first place if he'd thought it all through. His life was well ordered and relatively sane, and he planned to keep it that way.

"Excuse me," he said. "I have to rejoin my party."

"I didn't mean to keep you." The woman held out her hand, and what could he do but take it? "Thanks for rescuing my hat."

The scent of gardenia wafted off her skin, his favorite fragrance. "Of course," he said, or was it *You're welcome?*

Before the woman could play any more tricks on him, he hurried off with all his anonymity and most of his dignity intact.

"She's gorgeous," Aunt Dolly said the minute he sat down. "Lively, too. You can always tell."

His mother got right to the point. "Did you get her phone number?"

"I didn't even get her name."

"Ellie says she's a sweet girl." Kitty adjusted her liquor-advertisement hat. "She's not only a great photographer, she's an artist specializing in portraits."

Matt didn't care if she specialized in Kama Sutra, he still didn't want to know her name.

"She studied art in Paris," Kitty added. "Her name is Sandi Wentworth."

"I have to be going." Matt pushed his chair back, then leaned down to kiss his mother's cheek.

"Don't rush off," she said. "Ellie and Sam just got back. He's fixing to toss the garter."

"I pity the poor unlucky fool who catches it."

Matt rushed off and had nearly gained safety, when the garter sailed through the air and smacked him in the back of the head. He kept on going. But not before he noticed that the garter was made of red feathers with something attached that looked suspiciously like a sequined phallus.

Who would have thought Ellie Jones was that kind? And at her age. It just proved his theory: women were a devious lot bent on man's total undoing.

"There wasn't a single man at your dad's wedding who made me tingle," Sandi told her best friend, and C. J. Garrett said, "Thank God."

The two of them were sitting in rocking chairs on

the front porch of C.J.'s childhood home holding cold glasses of lemonade to their heat-flushed cheeks and trying not to comment on the twenty-nine candles that blazed on the birthday cake beside them.

Every candle burned a hole in Sandi's heart. It was her birthday, and the only person in the whole world who remembered was C.J.

"You didn't have to get me a cake," Sandi said.

"I wanted to." C.J. retrieved a small gift-wrapped box from the pocket of her sundress and handed it to Sandi. "Happy birthday."

"You shouldn't have."

"For Pete's sake, Sandi. You're like family to me."

It was true. The only real home Sandi had ever known was this warm yellow cottage next door to the cold house Sandi had inherited from the grandmother who had raised her, a stern, upright woman who had taught her everything about walking the straight and narrow and nothing about love.

The only real love she'd ever known had come from C.J. and her parents, Sam and Phoebe. She'd basked in the reflected glow for years, and truth to tell, that's still what she was doing.

C.J. was a newlywed and had been matron of honor as her widowed dad had just married his long-ago sweetheart, Ellie. If Sandi shut her eyes, she could almost smell the sweet scent of requited love wafting on the breeze that ruffled the roses on the trellis behind the swing.

"Aren't you going to open it?"

Sandi carefully peeled back the paper, folded it into

a neat square then opened the little black-velvet box. Nestled inside was a delicate necklace with a filigreed gold heart.

"Oh, it's beautiful, C.J. Thank you."

"I put pictures of you and me inside." Sandi popped open the clasp and on one side saw a photo of two gangly-legged kids with their arms draped around each other. On the opposite side was a close-up shot of them mugging for the camera, their faces smeared with chocolate icing and hope.

"My thirteenth birthday," Sandi said. She remembered it well. The day she'd turned teenager she'd waited all day by the telephone, certain her mother would call. "You might as well give up," her grandmother had told her. "Meredith's too busy with her new husband to bother with you. Take what you've got and be satisfied."

What she'd got was a new toothbrush wrapped in tinfoil and a curt "You can't be too careful about hygiene" from her grandmother.

Right before dark, C.J. and her parents had burst through the front door bearing a chocolate cake with thirteen candles, a pile of gifts in bright-purple paper and hugs enough to fill the empty spot in Sandi's heart.

She traced the wistful smile on the face of her younger self.

"Sisters forever," C.J. said, then fastened the delicate gold chain around Sandi's neck.

She placed her hand over the gold heart. "Sisters forever," she said.

"Clint and I are going to name our first child after you."

"You're pregnant?"

"Not yet, but we're hoping. Clint says there's no need to wait until I finish vet school. He'll set up a nursery in his newspaper office and take care of the baby while I'm in class."

Sandi wanted a family of her own more than anything, but first she had to find a husband. And that meant falling in love with somebody who would love her right back.

"I'm happy for you, C.J." And she was. Truly, she was.

C.J. squeezed her hands. "It'll happen for you, Sandi. I feel it in my bones."

"It takes two."

"You've been looking for love in the wrong places. Why don't you look at somebody smart and successful and steady instead of bullfighters and out of work artists? Somebody like Matt Coltrane? You ought to try to get to know him. He looks like a man with potential."

"No, he's not my type."

"How do you know?"

"I can tell by his uptight behavior."

"Ellie says he's very good to his mother. That speaks well of him."

"He doesn't jingle my chimes."

"I give up. Make a wish, Sandi."

She closed her eyes and wished for babies with

sweet pink faces. Then she blew out the candles. All twenty-nine of them.

The jangle of the telephone rousted Matt out of a deep sleep. He never dreamed. Dreams were too messy.

"Matt?"

"Aunt Dolly?" He glanced at the clock. Midnight. With no transition between sleeping and waking, he reached for his pants.

"You've got to come home. Lucy's had a heart attack."

"I'm on my way." He did a quick calculation. His bags were still packed, his gas tank full and his affairs in order. "I'll be there in three hours and sixteen minutes. How bad is it?"

"She overextended herself with the wedding. Kitty tried to tell her, but would she listen? Naturally not, you know how she is. And then, of course, she's always climbing the stairs when she could take the elevator. I don't know why she insists on sleeping upstairs when she could have her pick of bedrooms on the first floor."

"Aunt Dolly..."

"And then, of course, she *insisted* on having a private party for the Foxes after the wedding...."

"Aunt Dolly, is she dying?"

"God only knows."

Much as he loved Dolly Wilder, Matt couldn't help being exasperated with her. Sometimes she carried drama to the extreme. Why hadn't Aunt Kitty called him? She always cut straight to the point.

He'd hold off calling his sisters until he saw his mother's condition for himself. No sense in unduly alarming them. Anyway, neither of them could get home quickly. Kat was backpacking in Peru and Elizabeth was filming a documentary in Wales.

"Tell Mother I'm on my way."

"She'll be so relieved. I'm staying, of course. I've called London to get a replacement for the play. Not that they can ever replace me...."

"Aunt Dolly. I have to leave now. Tell Mother I'm coming home."

Dolly entered Lucy O'Banyon Coltrane's bedroom as if it were a Broadway stage. "Matt's on his way."

Lucy sighed. "Unfortunately, I'm not dying."

"Not dying!"

"Ben just left. He said it was nothing but a bad case of indigestion. We shot off the gun too soon."

"Good God." Dolly sank into a chair. Naturally she chose the pink-satin chaise longue. "What are we going to do?"

"We're going to call Matt on his cell phone and tell him not to come," said Kitty. "That's what we're going to do."

Trust Kitty to be practical. The only thing Lucy hated more than making a fool of herself in public was making a fool of herself in front of her children. Here was Matt, the busiest attorney in Jackson, driving all the way back to Shady Grove to chase a wild goose his mother had turned loose.

"Let me think," she said.

"What's to think about?" Kitty said. "For Pete's sake, you've got to tell him the truth."

"Not necessarily."

"Whatever plot you're hatching, I want no part of it," Kitty said.

Lucy didn't bother to deny she was hatching a plot. Why should she? She was a romance novelist, for goodness' sake. "Do you remember my tenth book, *Made-To-Order Bride*?"

"Tell me you're not thinking what I think you're thinking," Kitty said.

"Why not? Here's the way I see it. Matt's already picked out a woman."

"What woman?" Dolly asked.

"The one by the pool. The artist. Sandi Wentworth."

Kitty sniffed. "He didn't pick her out. He said she wasn't his type."

"Nobody's his type. My son's a stick-in-the-mud. If I don't give connubial bliss a little boost he's never going to be happy." Lucy's best plots always fell into her lap, so to speak. That's how she knew she'd hatched a humdinger. "Here's how it will work. I'll invite her here to paint my final portrait for my children and my fans.…"

"You're not dying," Kitty pointed out.

"A minor detail."

"He'll find out the truth as soon as he questions Ben," Kitty added.

"Ben will evade Matt if I ask him to." Ben Appleton was not only the family doctor who had been her husband Henry's partner in their medical practice, but a lifelong friend. "All we need is a few days. Two weeks at most. When Matt finally finds out I'm not dying, he'll be so happy he'll forget the little white lie I told."

"More like an encyclopedia of lies," Kitty said.

"We've done it before." They both glanced at Dolly who was busy pouring three glasses of wine. "The garden's full of herbs. Kitty, didn't you used to make a little love potion?"

"That was a long time ago," Kitty protested, but Lucy could tell by the look on her sister-in-law's face that she had won.

Dolly passed around the wine. "May this rescue be as dramatic and successful as the first."

They all lifted their glasses. "To the Foxes," they said.

Chapter Two

Sandi couldn't wait to get to Shady Grove. Though she usually obeyed speed laws, she drove over the limit all the way so she could arrive at O'Banyon Manor before dark. The mansion had so much family history.

No matter what its style, the mansion had a fairy-tale charm. She was going to love working here.

Lucille Coltrane had seemed nice on the phone, too. Warm and friendly. The kind of woman you feel you know after one conversation.

C.J. had told her that Kitty O'Banyon lived in the house as well, and that Dolly Wilder visited so often she might as well live there. All three women were her mother's friends.

"Kitty's an herbalist. She used to have a little shop

that sold the neatest things. Natural-healing oils and sleep masks filled with lavender. She grew up on a farm. Mom used to say if you wanted to know something, just ask Kitty.''

Sandi looked forward to cozy evenings chatting with Kitty O'Banyon. A woman like that who knew about domestic matters such as cooking and milking cows and pickling eggs might give her a tip or two on selecting a domesticated man. Or at least one already leash trained, one who would heel at the sound of the wedding march.

Heaven only knew, Sandi needed advice. And she needed it quick, before her rapidly aging eggs got too old.

Sandi was going to have fun in this house full of women—girl talk, laughter and tears.

She parked her 1960 baby-blue Thunderbird convertible underneath a magnolia tree, grabbed her duffel bag and art supplies, then bounded up the steps to ring the doorbell.

The door swung open, and there stood the hunk who had rescued her hat only three days earlier. When he saw her bag, he gave her a scowl.

''Yes?''

His tone of voice would frost toes. Sandi refused to be frosted.

''Hi, I'm Sandi Wentworth, and I'm here to paint Lucille Coltrane's portrait.''

''Your timing is off, Ms. Wentworth. My mother is a very sick woman and in no condition to pose for you.''

"Oh, I won't ask her to pose. I'll merely sit with her a little each day, get to know her features, her personality. She won't have to do a thing except lie in bed. I can even feed her broth and read to her, if you like."

"Perhaps I haven't made myself clear. You won't be doing any of those things. Good day, Ms. Wentworth."

Sandi had seen people in movies stick their foot in a closing door, but she'd never thought she would be one of those people. She was deciding whether to sacrifice her right or her left foot, when a stunning woman with flaming titian hair and a bright-red blouse tucked into her jeans appeared in the doorway.

"You must be Sandi," she said. "Please do come inside."

Sandi cast a suspicious eye toward the guardian dragon. "Are you sure it's all right?"

"Don't mind him. That's Lucy's son, Matt. His bark is worse than his bite." The woman took her bag and handed it to the crown prince of intimidation. "Take her bag upstairs, Matt. The pink room in the east wing. And stop that scowling. It'll give you wrinkles. At your advancing age you don't need any more of them."

The woman grabbed Sandi's hand and practically dragged her into the hallway. "I'm Dolly Wilder."

She lifted an eyebrow, and Sandi took her cue. "The star of stage and screen. I'm delighted to meet you, Ms. Wilder."

"Please, call me Dolly." She raised her voice and

added, "Or Aunt Dolly, if you wish. That's what Matt calls me." If he heard he didn't let on. "Oh, Kitty...look who's here."

Kitty O'Banyon had come from the back of the house swathed in a white apron. At first glance she appeared to be a plain woman without a single redeeming feature. But she had the kind of strong, arresting face you couldn't look away from. Sandi still remembered it from the wedding. Up close she saw the wide-set gray eyes and a generous mouth that might have been pretty if she'd bothered with makeup.

"We're delighted to have you with us." Her greeting was far more reserved than Dolly's, but her smile was genuine. "I hope you like rack of lamb with rosemary and mint."

"It sounds delicious, but I don't want to intrude on a family meal. I'll just pop downtown and get a hamburger."

"Absolutely not!" Dolly said.

Kitty added, "I love to cook, and we usually have food going to waste. I hope you'll eat all your meals with us while you're here."

"Thank you. You're more than generous." Considering the circumstances, their festive air surprised Sandi.

As if she'd read her thoughts, Dolly put on a long face. "Poor Lucy, of course, won't be joining us."

"No," Kitty said, her own face drawn downward. "Poor Lucy."

Dolly brightened. "You just have time to freshen up. Let me show you to your room."

Sandi followed Dolly Wilder across a cavernous ballroom, through several ornate sitting rooms and hallways then up a winding staircase.

"I hope I don't get lost," she said.

"If you do, just ask Matt. He's in the room next to yours."

Great, only a wall to separate her from the man who never smiled. She hoped he didn't give her nightmares.

After Dolly left her, Sandi wished she'd asked exactly what was meant by *freshen up*. Did they dress for dinner? Certainly the surroundings called for full makeup and a fancy dress. The fact that the owner of the mansion was near death could change things, though. Perhaps Dolly only meant wash your face and comb your hair.

On the other hand, Dr. Darkness would be there, probably still in his three-piece suit and tie. He acted as if he hated her already. There was no reason to give him further cause.

Besides, you never knew when the opportunity to find a husband would strike.

Remembering Matt Coltrane's scowl, she shuddered. "Please, God, don't let opportunity strike here."

She settled on a great-looking little black dress, then swept her long hair into a French knot with flyaway tendrils.

She got lost twice before she finally found the dining room, which was filled with a delicious spread of food. She noticed that Matt was absent.

"Matt decided to eat with his mother," Dolly said. "He offered his apologies."

Sandi doubted that, but she was too polite to say so. "I'm sorry she's so ill," she said taking a seat at the table.

"How kind of you. Matt's brilliant, you know," Dolly added, taking a seat and glaring at Kitty.

"Ouch," Kitty said, smiling. "Lucy's son is a top-notch divorce attorney. She's very proud of him. We all are."

"Rich," Dolly said. "I'm surprised some lucky girl hasn't already run off with him. Have some more mint sauce, Sandi. It's good for you."

"I made it with fresh herbs from the garden." Kitty's whole face lit up when she spoke of her garden. Sandi seized the opportunity to steer the conversation toward domestic matters.

"It's delicious. I'd love to make a garden in my backyard. I just don't know if I have enough room for a garden as well as a playground for the children."

"You have children?" Kitty seemed excited about the idea and looked disappointed when Sandi shook her head.

"Not yet. I'd like a big family someday, though."

"Good." Dolly acted as if the whole brood would be born for her benefit. "Matt adores children, too. He's quite a Romeo, you know. It wouldn't surprise me if he fathers five or six."

"More mint sauce, dear?" Kitty picked up the bowl and ladled it onto Sandi's plate before Sandi could protest that she couldn't eat another bite.

"He's a real Casanova," Dolly said.

"Wasn't Casanova unscrupulous?" The words flew out of Sandi's mouth before she could stop them. To make matters worse, she added, "I've had it with men of that sort."

What in the world was wrong with her? She knew better. She hadn't even touched her wine. One sip made her tipsy and half a glass shot her over the moon. She looked down at her plate as if it might provide answers, but all she saw was the sick green sauce swimming all over her half-eaten lamb.

"Well, naturally I didn't mean anything of the sort about Matt." Dolly didn't seem to be taking offense, which made Sandi feel better. "He knows a lot about romance, that's all. He's true blue, as good as gold, salt of the earth, cream of the crop."

"One bad metaphor was more than enough, Dolly." Kitty picked up the damnable bowl of mint sauce. "More sauce, dear?"

Sandi shielded her plate with both hands. "No, please. Any more of that and I'll be dancing on the table in my black-lace thong."

"You're wearing a lace thong?" Dolly clapped her hands. "That's absolutely perfect for romance."

It hadn't worked for Sandi yet, but she wasn't so far gone she planned to admit defeat in the romance department.

"What time is it?" Kitty looked at her watch, and Dolly jumped up from the table.

"Bedtime."

"It's only eight-thirty," Sandi said, which wasn't

like her at all. Such bad manners. Her grandmother would be spinning in her grave.

"We go to bed early, don't we, Kitty?"

"With the chickens."

Kitty cleared the table while Dolly linked arms with Sandi and led her into a walnut-paneled room with cozy chintz furniture and bookshelves filled with interesting-looking books. Lucy's romances occupied two whole shelves.

Every single one of the titles made Sandi feel inadequate. *You Plus Me Equals Love, Love Is All We've Got, Love Is Bustin' Out All Over,* just to name a few. All that printed passion made her dizzy, and she had to sit down.

"Help yourself to anything in the library." Dolly sashayed to the desk and came back with a deck of cards. "You might want to play some cards."

"I don't play solitaire. It seems so lonely, somehow."

"I was thinking of strip poker." She patted Sandi's arm. "Well, good night dear. We'll send Matt down to make sure you can find your way to your room."

More than likely he would show her the door…unless she could think of some way to win him over so she could complete the portrait she'd been commissioned to do. Perhaps if she asked his advice, appealed to his ego. Men liked that.

There she was, curled up in a chintz chair waiting for him like a black widow spider. In *his* favorite chair, to boot. Posing, for God's sake. Pretending to read a book. She sat with one foot tucked under her, head tilted exactly right so the lamp would shine on those little strands of hair so artfully draped against her cheek.

Matt was going to kill Kitty and Dolly. They'd stopped by his mother's room and announced they were off to bed and he should escort their guest to her room.

He could have pointed out that Dolly never went to bed till midnight and that Sandi Wentworth was not his guest, but he didn't want to make a scene in front of his mother. She was so weak she was barely coherent. He couldn't get a thing out of her except, "It's my heart, son."

Aunt Dolly was no better, which didn't surprise Matt. She was known for beauty not brains. But Kitty was a different story. Usually she was articulate and sensible. He supposed his mother's condition had her so upset she couldn't think straight. After all, they were as close as sisters.

Why had Ben Appleton gone out of town and left his mother in that condition? It wasn't like him to be so careless. He was the one Matt really wanted to talk to. And he would, even if he had to storm the travel agency to find out where Ben had gone.

But first he had to deal with the enticing little tramp sitting in his chair.

"Your book's upside down."

She gave a guilty start, then batted her big eyes at him. For a moment he almost forgot she was a shameless vixen. Green eyes ought to be outlawed.

"Oh, I didn't hear you come in."

Darned if she didn't put her hand over her chest. Another nasty ploy. All those pearly-pink nails resting on those nicely rounded little breasts.

Matt strolled casually across the room then whirled back and sat in the chair next to hers. He stretched so far his knee rested against her leg.

She jerked back as if he'd branded her with a hot poker. That would teach her to try to outfox a warhorse. He'd had years of practice in keeping his opponents off balance.

"I see you were *reading* one of my mother's books."

"Yes, I was trying to learn."

"Learn what?"

"About love. I'm a miserable failure at it." She did that *thing* with her eyes again.

"I doubt that."

"Really, I am. Of course, I didn't expect much from my first fiancé. Pierre was the artistic type."

Wimpy. Weak. Matt pictured him with a certain malicious glee.

Sandi leaned toward him and he almost missed the false earnestness on her face because of the low cut of her dress.

"My second one didn't have any staying power," she said.

Probably some wealthy old geezer who needed Viagra. Clearly she'd been trying to kill him with sex.

"Raoul was a bullfighter." Matt's image of the old

geezer died an ignominious death. "I think he'd had one too many close calls with a bull."

"Maybe you'll have better luck next time," he said.

"Oh, but I didn't. My third fiancé…"

"Your third?"

"Yes."

"How many fiancés have you had?"

"Three."

She was worse than Matt had imagined. She had to be…what? Twenty-four? Twenty-five? At the rate she was going, she'd decimate the entire bachelor population before she was forty-five.

He had a sudden vision of her on a worldwide husband hunt, selecting and discarding poor unsuspecting males the way she would cheap baubles for her charm bracelet. He applauded himself that he had more sense than to be among that number.

"I suppose you have number four all picked out?"

"Oh, no. That's the problem. I don't seem to have the right touch with men."

If she leaned any farther, she was going to fall out of her chair. Or pop out of her dress. Too bad all that beautiful cleavage had to be wasted on a man-eating floozy.

"Can you educate me?" she said.

He thought he'd heard every line, but this was a new one. He couldn't wait to see how far she would go.

"I'm afraid I don't follow you."

"You're an expert. Maybe you can give me a few pointers."

"I deal with love's demise, not its birth."

"Still, you know things about the way men think."

"Obviously. I'm a man."

Appearing completely artless, she made a clever movement and one of her straps slid off her shoulder. "Do I arouse you?"

Caught red-handed. Or steel-rodded, as the case happened to be. The scary thing about his condition was that Matt hadn't even noticed when the power shifted from him to her.

"You can stop playing this game, Ms. Wentworth. Your little tricks won't work on me."

"Little tricks? How dare you say such a thing! And I was trying to be so nice."

She jumped out of her chair, then toppled. Matt caught her with the ease he'd caught pigskin on the high-school football field. She wrapped her arms around his neck and melted all over him in a kittenish display of innocent seduction.

He gritted his teeth. "I should have let you fall."

"Why didn't you?" The cute little kitten turned to a tigress. Next she would be unsheathing her claws.

"Because I'm a gentleman."

"You're no gentleman." She shoved at him, then looked up big-eyed and said, "Unhand me," exactly like one of the heroines Dolly had played in B-grade movies.

"Gladly." He released her, and she teetered toward the left.

This time he didn't just catch her around the waist, he scooped her up and threw her over his shoulder.

All night she'd been asking for a caveman, and that's exactly what she was going to get.

"Put me down." She battered his back with her fists.

"You've had too much to drink." He marched toward the door and snapped off the lights on the way out of the library. No sense wasting electricity.

"I don't drink."

"That's a likely story." The spitfire didn't bite back. "Or maybe it's the truth. Maybe this is all part of your act."

She still didn't take the bait. Never mind, the front door lay just ahead. He would dump her outside and be done with her.

"This is the end of the line for you, Ms. Wentworth. You'll have to find some other sucker to deceive." She was still playing possum. "Ms. Wentworth." He gave her backside a sharp pat. "Sandi, wake up. Game's over."

Dead silence. Plus, she was a dead weight. Matt slid her off his shoulder and she lolled sideways in his arms.

"Shoot." She'd passed out. *Now* what was he going to do?

Lucy and Dolly and Kitty were propped up against Lucy's headboard with their feet in fuzzy bed socks while they watched a rerun of Cary Grant and Deborah Kerr in *An Affair to Remember*.

"Are you sure everything went all right at dinner?" Lucy asked. "You were subtle, weren't you?"

"Yes," Dolly said, and Kitty snorted. "What about all that mint sauce you gave her?" Dolly retorted.

"Do you think I put a little too much muscadine wine in it?"

"What about my pie?" Lucy said. "And while you're gone, check to see how the lovebirds are doing."

"What if they catch me?"

"Sneak, Kitty," Dolly said. *"Sneak."*

When Kitty got back, she said, "It looks like a Mexican standoff down there."

"Is that good or bad?" Lucy asked.

Dolly, who was the expert of the three on account of her many love affairs, pronounced the verdict.

"It could go either way."

Chapter Three

If he didn't have such a tender heart Matt would bundle the vixen into her car, toss her duffel bag in behind her. Then, when she got sober enough to drive, she'd be out of his mother's house and out of his life. In spite of the fact his opponents in court and more than one woman had accused him of being heartless, Matt was really a soft touch.

He couldn't simply dump her outside. She might be scared of the dark.

Sighing, he trudged up the staircase that had never seemed longer, wondering why this little vamp had to come in such an enticing package.

"Here we go." When he reached her room, he shifted her off his shoulder and into his arms, then laid her out on the bed as if he were arranging a display of fine diamonds.

She wore a little black dress and not much else. Her feet were small and high-arched with toes as delicate as fine porcelain, toenails painted purple.

Matt stalked to the closet and dragged out a quilt to cover her before he made any more unsettling discoveries. In the short time it took him to get back to the bed, she'd shifted so that her skirt was hiked up to Christmas and her top was barely covering her.

Desire stabbed him so hard he was actually in pain. Gritting his teeth, he tossed the quilt over her. Unfortunately it flopped over her face and he had to adjust the covers so she could breathe.

She sighed, her breath soft and warm against his hand. Riveted, Matt watched her face. Nothing was more appealing than a sleeping beautiful woman.

Against his will he touched her cheek. No person had ever exerted such power over him. Matt forced himself to back away from her bed.

"Sleep tight, little succubus. Tomorrow you get your walking papers."

He escaped to his own bedroom, tossing and turning all night with dreams of being caught in the web of a golden spider with eyes the color of the sea.

The next morning, the sun slapped Matt in the face. He bolted upright and glared at the clock. It had to be wrong. He never slept past six. Occasionally he indulged himself on a weekend and slept till six-thirty, but *eight?*

"Damn," he said. Here he was lying abed while Sandi Wentworth had full range of the house. Even

worse, she had time to exert her strange and mesmer-
izing power over his mother. It didn't take much to
fool Lucy. That's why it was imperative that he get
that enticing vixen out of the house. Today.

Matt jerked on his clothes and didn't even bother
to shave. A first for him. Rapping on the connecting
door between their bedrooms, he called her name.
"Ms. Wentworth? Are you up?"

No answer. Which turned out to be a very good
thing, for Matt Coltrane had done the unthinkable.
He'd forgotten to put on his shoes.

"Damn," he said once more. Not only did he put
on his shoes—he shaved. What did fifteen more
minutes hurt?

He knocked again, the hall door this time. He wasn't
about to get trapped inside a bedroom with her. Fifteen
minutes had given him time to regain his composure.
Another first for him. He *never* lost composure.

"Sandi. Rise and shine." When he got no response,
he pushed open the door. The bed was neatly made
and her duffel was out of sight. The only evidence that
she had been there was the perfume that lingered in
the air, that heady fragrance that was going to be his
undoing.

Matt backed out of the room and hurried to the west
wing to have a heart-to-heart talk with his mother.
Portrait or no portrait, Sandi had to go.

"Mother," he said, and Lucy held up a hand.
"Shh," she said. "Sandi's at the good part."

The vixen sat on the side of the bed, transformed.
She was wearing a little blue-and-white sundress with

an honest-to-God sailor collar. She looked like a schoolgirl of sixteen. Totally innocent. Never been kissed.

"Good morning, Matt." Her smile lit the whole room.

He didn't smile back. Didn't dare. "Morning." He gave her a curt nod, then skirted around her so he could kiss Lucy's cheek. "How are you feeling this morning, Mother?"

"Much better now that Sandi's reading to me."

He glanced at the book—*Gone With The Wind.* Wouldn't you know? A thousand pages. And she was on page ten.

"You don't have to do that, Ms. Wentworth."

"Oh, but I don't mind. In fact, I love it."

"So do I. Sit down, Matt, and stop scowling."

"I need to go to the bank and get papers for you to sign, Mother."

"Kitty's gone to do that." Lucy patted the bed. "Sit down and visit a minute."

He sat on the edge of the bed and took his mother's hand. The sight of her red-painted fingernails almost broke his heart. Lucy had always been so full of life. It didn't seem possible that she was dying.

"Where's Aunt Dolly?"

"Gone to buy Chinese lanterns."

"Chinese lanterns?"

"To swing across the courtyard." Lucy stroked his hand. "Don't look so disapproving. I thought a festive alfresco dinner with music would do us all a world of good."

"Music?"

"Yes. Dolly's hiring a band."

"Good God, Mother, you're not up to a party."

"I know, dear, but it will make me feel better to think of the rest of you having a good time."

Matt became unsettled just thinking about being around Sandi Wentworth in the romantic setting.

"I think Ms. Coltrane looks better already," Sandi said. "Just look at the roses in her cheeks."

"That's the flush of sickness." He strode across the room, as far as possible from Sandi. "Ms. Wentworth, I need to talk to you. Alone."

Lucy pouted. "She's not finished reading. I want her to read, and I want you to go downstairs and fetch me a nice cool glass of lemonade. Bring one for Sandi, too."

As he stalked out, his mother said, "He's not really such a bear."

Sandi said, "I know. Underneath that gruff exterior he's kind of sweet."

Sweet? Sweet! The next thing he knew she'd be tying a pink ruffled apron on him and calling him *domestic*.

As he poured lemonade he thought about Chinese lanterns, moonlight and music. "Turn your back for one minute," he muttered.

He would have to be more vigilant. While the cat wasn't watching, the mice had revolted and were threatening to take over.

He'd have to a build a mousetrap, that was all. And he knew the perfect one....

* * *

Sandi needed advice, and she needed it now. She called C.J.

"C.J., I'm in love."

"Not again. Who is it this time?"

"Not *who*. I'm in love with this house. My room has the greatest old four-poster bed, walnut. The canopy is crocheted, hand done. I keep picturing myself lying there with a baby. Matt's baby."

"Matt? As in Matt Coltrane?"

"Yes."

"That's wonderful."

"That's terrible. He hates me."

"Sandi, nobody hates you. You're sweet and wonderful and kind. You're smart and beautiful...."

"He thinks I'm a tramp."

C.J. started laughing.

"I don't see what's so funny."

"Men. The harder they fall, the faster they run."

"You mean, he pretends he hates me because he likes me?"

"Yes. Some people are scared of love, Sandi. Clint was."

"I remember that. But you were always in love with him. I'm not in love with Matt. Just his house. Though he is wonderful to his mother. This morning she asked for lemonade, and he brought roses, too. He picked them in the garden. Don't you think that's kind of sweet?"

"I do."

"And then he kept saying he had to leave and take care of her business affairs, but he puttered around her desk the whole time I was reading to Lucy. I get goose bumps just thinking about his stolen glances.''

"Stolen glances? You've been reading romance."

"Yes. One of Lucy's. Tender Is The Plight." Sandi's skin flushed thinking about romance and love and babies and Matt. Especially Matt. "Tonight there'll be a band and Chinese lanterns and a full moon. Oh, C.J., what am I going to do?"

She supposed she sounded desperate, and maybe she was. How many chances did a girl get? Besides, she wasn't even sure she wanted a romance with Matt Coltrane. She wanted a man to adore her. She wanted a man to love her every moment of every day, no matter what. She wanted love requited and unconditional.

"Don't do anything, Sandi. Don't try to figure angles, don't play games. Just be yourself. Be honest and follow your heart. The universe will take care of the rest."

In the background she could hear Clint's deep voice then C.J.'s soft, muffled giggle. Sandi felt guilty taking her away from her husband with idle chatter about her own problems.

"Thank you, C.J. Tell Clint hello for me. Sorry I kept you so long."

"Call anytime, Sandi. I mean that. Call me."

"Okay."

Sinking into the deep comforting folds of the bed, Sandi imagined herself in a pink satin bed jacket, continuing her dream.

* * *

Mood music drifted up from the courtyard, and from his window Matt could see Sandi Wentworth in the soft glow of Chinese lanterns. Wearing white. Looking demure and virginal and helpless.

"How am I going to force her to show her true colors with her looking like that?"

He'd expected vampish red with slits that showed lots of leg and a plunging neckline that showed lots of breast. Not that soft, diaphanous skirt that made her look as if she was walking on a cloud. Not that high neckline that showed not a single shred of cleavage.

"She looks like a bride."

Matt was furious. He jerked on his tuxedo jacket and raced downstairs. Before dinner got cold. Before he could change his mind.

"Matt." Good God. Sandi practically *glowed* when she said his name.

To make matters worse, she touched his cheek. Once. Briefly. A butterfly's brush that lingered just long enough for him to be almost overcome with that siren's fragrance that wafted off her hair, her skin. What diabolical game was she playing now?

"I thought you weren't coming," she said.

"I never miss dinner."

"Oh."

She feigned disappointment so well, he almost believed her.

"Will you excuse me? I have to talk with Aunt Kitty." He left Sandi beside a potted hibiscus and bolted toward a fountain.

"Aunt Kitty." Matt was so happy to be in safe territory, he practically fawned over his startled aunt.

"Why, Matt. What's put you in such an expansive mood?"

"Our guest, I hope," Dolly said.

"She's not my guest. She's mother's."

Dolly swatted him arm with her Japanese fan, a theatrical touch she'd added to her long embroidered silk kimono. "You're more fun when you smile."

"I'm smiling." He made a grimace in her direction, and was turning to ask Kitty about the papers from the bank, when Dolly grabbed her arm and raced toward the wrought iron table. "Matt," she called over her shoulder, "escort Miss Wentworth to dinner."

What had gotten into her? Dolly Wilder's manners had always been impeccable. Was she getting senile? At this early age?

Sandi gave him that megawatt smile again. He could almost believe it was genuine.

"It looks like we're stuck with each other for the duration." He offered his arm. "May I?"

"Of course. How lovely."

"That's a strange word for torture."

"Do you plan to torture me?"

Artless. That's what she seemed. Too bad it was all an act.

"Yes."

He tried to conjure up images of her slowly roasting on a spit, but all he saw was Sandi spilled across the bed with the moon in her hair and his lips on her skin. Rapturous torture. Exquisite torture.

"Then I must warn you. I'm the screaming type."

Matt suppressed a groan. He would have to be more careful. This woman was an expert. Get her in a court of law, and he would make mincemeat of her. But put her in the bedroom and he was out of his league.

He'd avoided that venue for years, and he didn't plan on taking any crash courses now.

"My victims don't scream, Ms. Wentworth. They run."

She laughed. Darned if she didn't throw back her head to boot. The moon gilded her throat and the Chinese lanterns shot golden sparks off her hair.

My God, she was the most beautiful woman he'd ever seen. The most appealing. And the most dangerous.

"I'm not the running type," she said.

"Another warning?"

"No, just an honest confession. You see, I grew up the hard way, Matt. My dad died when I was three, and I was brought up by a series of nannies who trotted me out to play *cute* for whichever current lover my mother wanted to impress. After I got too old to be cute, she packed me off to live with my grandmother who subscribed to the creed 'out of sight, out of mind.' Little children were to be washed and fed and put to bed without fanfare and as quickly as possible. My mom's friend Phoebe provided the only touch of home I ever knew."

Matt felt poleaxed. He wanted to fold her into his arms and hold her tight and whisper sweet encouragement against her hair. He wanted to tuck her into warm blankets and bring her hot chocolate and stroke her beautiful face while he told her how very much she was loved.

He must be going crazy. Speechless, he stood in the middle of his mother's courtyard listening to the distant call of whippoorwills and trying to pack ice back around his heart.

"I'm sorry," she whispered. "I didn't mean to blurt out those things. It just happened. There's something about you..."

He put his hand on her cheek. That was all. Just put it there and let it rest for a moment, warm and loving and reassuring.

"It's okay, Sandi." Her smile carried a world of bravery and a hint of tears. "It's okay."

She nodded, and Matt put his hand on her elbow and led her to the table where Dolly and Kitty waited, led her with such care, he feared the thawing of his heart would become a permanent condition.

His carefully laid plans went up in smoke. How could he try to get Sandi to reveal her true colors when she was a rainbow?

The things she'd said had the ring of veracity, and yet he'd been fooled before. Not for one evening, but for several months. He'd have sworn that his fiancée was the real thing, an angel-faced woman of sweet temperament and honorable intentions. And yet Nancy McMains Stayman had turned out to be a gold-digging floozy with the heart of a barracuda.

And then there had been that awful and shocking

revelation about his dad, a man Matt had once considered a hero.

No, he couldn't afford to stick around. He would get through dinner as quickly as possible, then make his escape.

When they reached the table, he breathed a sigh of relief. But even after he pulled out Sandi's chair, his hands still burned with the print of her soft skin.

"Oh, everything looks wonderful," she said. "I haven't eaten alfresco since I was in Paris."

"You studied there, didn't you?" Dolly said.

"Yes. Even when I was a toddler I knew I wanted to paint. Fortunately, Dad was the kind of man who planned ahead. 'Someday you will study at the Sorbonne,' he used to say, and then he made sure I could. He was a wonderful man. I remember he used to carry me outside on his shoulders to watch rainbows."

"Is that why so many of your paintings feature rainbows?" Dolly asked.

Matt had thought Sandi was merely a photographer and a portrait painter. He had no idea that she had a body of work. Trust Dolly to know, though. There was hardly a topic she couldn't discuss, hardly a current event she didn't know about or had witnessed in her travels.

He found himself leaning toward Sandi, waiting for her answer with more than idle curiosity.

"Yes," she said. "Not only are rainbows pure, untouched beauty and symbolic of promise, but they evoke memories of family for me. Happy memories."

Matt pictured Sandi riding high above the crowd on

her daddy's shoulders, laughing with the freedom and uninhibited delight of a child. And he had a sudden, unexpected desire to make her laugh that way again.

"Will you excuse me, please?" He pushed back his chair and stood up.

"Matt, you haven't even eaten your dinner." This from Aunt Kitty. Worried.

"I'm going to take my plate up and eat with Mother. She's probably getting lonesome. Good night, all."

"Good night, Matt," Sandi said, and then she set about blaming herself for his leaving. If she'd talked about happy, uplifting things instead of her painful past, he would have stayed.

Then she got ashamed of herself for wanting him to stay. She was selfish to the core, wanting to keep a man by her side while his mother lay upstairs dying. But, oh, she had enjoyed the touch of his hand upon her cheek. She'd loved the way he held her elbow, the solid feel of him as he walked beside her, the sense of power and confidence that emanated from him as he sat beside her at the table.

She got through dinner but didn't know how. Then as soon as she could, she made her own escape. But not to her room. She couldn't bear the thought of being alone in that wonderful four-poster bed.

Instead, she went into the library and got comfortable with a good book. But not one of Lucy's romances. Sandi couldn't bear to read about other people falling in love and having babies while her own arms and womb were so painfully empty.

Chapter Four

His mother's business affairs were a tangled mess. Matt felt guilty for letting them get that way. He pushed back from the desk that had belonged to his father, rubbed the back of his aching neck and noticed with some shock that it was after midnight.

If he could finish one more document tonight, then he could start tomorrow knowing that he'd made progress. The document he needed was in his mother's desk in her bedroom. He'd kicked off his tuxedo shoes an hour ago, and if he was careful, maybe he could sneak in and get what he needed without disturbing her.

Shoeless, he hurried to the west wing, then tiptoed down the hall toward Lucy's bedroom door. A thin line of light showed underneath. His mother had fallen asleep with the lamp on, poor dear.

"If the music and Chinese lanterns didn't do the trick, I don't know what will."

Matt stopped, stunned. Aunt Kitty was in his mother's bedroom. At this hour. She should know better.

He was all set to march in there and chastise her for keeping Lucy from her rest when he heard Aunt Dolly.

"You're being too hasty, Kitty. Didn't you see the way he was looking at her?"

Matt had a sneaking suspicion he knew who she was talking about. He couldn't keep his eyes off Sandi all evening. If he'd stayed any longer, he'd have devoured her on the spot.

"What I want to know," Lucy said, "is whether our plan is working."

Plan? They'd *planned* this?

"Is my son falling in love with Sandi Wentworth?"

"Yes," Dolly said.

"No," Kitty said.

"You don't know that, Kitty."

"Neither do you, Dolly Wilder. I *told* you we should mind our own business."

"Oh, please," Lucy said. "This is not about meddling. All I want is to see my son happy."

Matt's first thought was to storm into his mother's bedroom and confront her. But then he remembered her condition. She'd recently had a heart attack, she was fragile, and she was dying.

He hurried out of the west wing. The only good thing to come out of his unintentional eavesdropping was that now he had a legitimate reason to send Sandi Wentworth home.

He would tell her first thing in the morning. She'd be on her way by eight o'clock. Nine at the latest.

His stomach rumbled, reminding him of all that delicious food he'd left on the table, and he decided to make a quick detour to the kitchen. As he passed the library, he caught a glimpse of white.

Sandi, illuminated by lamp glow, sitting in his favorite chair. He moved closer. She was reading his favorite book—The Tao of Physics.

"Sandi." She jumped as if he'd startled her. Clever girl. "You're quite an actress, aren't you?"

"What? What in the world are you talking about?"

"All that sentimental garbage about your bad childhood. It was merely a ploy to gain my sympathy, wasn't it?"

Her face paled, and her shock looked genuine. Matt was almost sorry for her.

"That is probably the vilest, lowest thing anybody has ever said to me. I'm sorry I ever told you. And even sorrier I ever met you."

She was magnificent in her rage. Matt applauded. "Bravo, Ms. Wentworth. A performance worthy of Bette Davis in *Now, Voyager.*"

He'd cornered her, and now she was on the run. Matt blocked her escape.

"Move out of my way," she said.

"You don't get off that easy."

"If you don't step aside I'm going to…to…" Sandi sagged, the fight suddenly gone out of her. She covered her face with her hands and made a sound that nearly broke his heart. The heart he'd tried so hard to keep deep-frozen and safe.

"Oh," she gasped. "Oh…" She was crying in earnest and looked as if she might never stop.

"Sandi…Sandi…" Her shoulders shook, her whole body shook. "Look, I know I can be difficult sometimes. Heck, I'm difficult most of the time." She looked as if she was about to break apart. Alarmed, Matt touched her arm, and that's all it took.

Suddenly she was in his arms, her face pressed tightly against his chest, wetting the front of his tuxedo with her tears. He patted her shoulder, stroked her hair, smoothed her back.

Then magically everything changed. He was no longer comforting her, and she was no longer sobbing. They were touching and caressing, giving in, giving up, giving over to the powerful currents that arced between them.

Desire bloomed, fierce and urgent, as unwelcome as the sudden summer storms that sweep over O'Banyon Manor knocking out power lines and rendering the household helpless.

That's how Matt felt. Helpless. Totally defenseless against the onslaught of passion.

"I'm sorry," he said, and stepped back. Empty. Almost bereft.

She pushed back her golden curtain of hair and looked at him with still-wet eyes.

God, how many ways could this woman disarm him? "Let's start over, shall we?"

"Okay. Do I need to sit down?"

"Yes. Over there." If he touched her again, he was lost.

"This sounds serious."

"It is." Matt told her what he'd overheard, watching her face to see if she already knew. She didn't. There are certain ways you can tell if a person is lying, nervous mannerisms, shifting eyes, sweating. Sandi Wentworth passed his tests. All of them.

"You mean, Lucy and Kitty and Dolly brought me here so you and I would fall in love?"

"Yes."

Sandi sat quietly for a while, not even bothering to wipe the smudge of mascara off her cheek, not even aware. Matt found that endearing. And disturbing in ways he didn't want to acknowledge.

When she finally spoke, her voice was soft and tender. "How sweet."

"Is that what you call meddling? Sweet?"

"Think about it, Matt. Your mother is dying and her last wish is for you to be happy. Don't you find that endearing?"

"I find it exasperating. Look, Sandi. My mother brought you here under false pretenses. There's no way her plan is going to work."

"Oh, I completely agree."

"You do?"

"Of course. You're not my type."

Matt didn't want to be her type, did he? He was relieved, wasn't he?

"I'm glad we're in agreement," he said. "First

thing tomorrow I'll help you get your bag and art supplies to the car, and you can go home. I'll deal with Mother.''

''She'll be so disappointed.''

''She has to learn that she can't play around with the lives of other people. Life is not one of her romance novels.''

''But, Matt, wouldn't it be wonderful if we could grant her dying wish?''

''Fall in love?'' He would as soon try to fly to the moon...without wings.

''We could pretend.''

''I'm no good at pretending.''

''Just think how happy we could make your mother. Oh, do say *yes*, Matt.''

''Maybe,'' he said, meaning *no*. At her crestfallen look, he said, ''I'll think about it,'' knowing he would think of nothing else. When she gave him a radiant smile that warmed him all the way to his toes, he added, ''Tomorrow we'll see,'' meaning *yes*.

What could be so hard about pretending to fall in love with the kindest-hearted woman he'd ever met?

Matt stood in the middle of the library drunk on Sandi's lingering fragrance and dumbfounded by his own stupidity. Of all the insane things he'd ever done, pretending to fall in love topped the list. For one thing, the very idea of love made him cringe. For another, he didn't know the first thing about romancing a woman.

His ill-fated romance with the blessedly long-gone Nancy McMains Stayman proved that.

He glanced down at his feet. Things would have turned out differently if he'd been wearing shoes. A shoeless man is a defenseless man. A shoeless man can't be responsible for his actions.

What he would do was wait till morning, then tell Sandi he'd changed his mind.

And she'd get that forsaken look on her face, that little-girl-lost look that made him want to scoop her up, ensconce her on satin cushions and keep harm at bay with a gold-hilted sword.

"Damn," he muttered. He was losing his mind.

Come dawn, he would lose face as well. Matt hated being second-rate at anything. Even romance.

What he needed was a few lessons. What he needed was a crash course.

He'd just put his hand on the light switch, when he noticed his mother's novels occupying two complete shelves. He'd never read them, never wanted to. Naturally he was proud of her, even bragged about her talent whenever he got a chance, but he'd never had the least inclination to know what was between the covers of her books.

His secretary, Janice, called them things like *fantastic, amazingly romantic, steamy.* Matt stalked to the shelves and selected a handful. *Romantic* he could use. Maybe even *fantastic.* He didn't plan on letting his pretense advance to the steamy stage, but it never hurt to be prepared.

He hurried to the bedroom with his arsenal of seductive weapons, then locked the door. Picking up a book called *Penelope's Persuasion,* he turned to Chapter One....

Armed with a dagger in her stocking and her father's musket under her cloak, Penelope lifted the latch of the heavy wrought-iron gates that guarded Brentwood Manor and slipped into the darkness. Tonight Pierre Lafette would pay for what he'd stolen...the largest plantation in Louisiana and a maiden's virginity. *Her* virginity.

"Good lord," Matt said. He would hate to meet this Penelope creature in the dark. A man looking at the business end of a dagger and a musket could be persuaded of many things.

He tossed the book aside. Those were the wrong weapons for the kind of persuasion he had in mind.

Pawing through his pile of purloined romances, he selected another title. Matt opened the book called *Tenderness,* and began to read...

I'll never forget the day Jim proposed. He was kneeling on my doorstep with the rain pelting his bare head and his arms full of oranges, never mind that we were at the height of a depression and oranges were more precious than gold. "Cynthia, will you marry me?" he said, and I told him yes on the spot. We went inside to the parlor and...

Matt gave a satisfied grunt. "Now, that's more like it," he said. Employing the speed-reading technique he used to plow through tomes of legal documents, he finished the book before sleep claimed him. Couldn't put it down, as a matter of fact.

When he finally did, he sat in his rumpled tuxedo amazed. "Who would have thought Mother knew all that?"

Sandi nearly tripped on the oranges outside her bedroom door. There were twelve of them piled into a pewter bowl.

"What in the world?" Who would put oranges at her door?

She picked up the bowl. There was no note, no clue as to how the fruit came to be there. Maybe the housekeeper had been on her way to the library with them and had been interrupted. But that didn't make sense. Both the kitchen and the library were on the first floor.

Mystified, Sandi picked up the bowl and carried it along with her art supplies to the west wing. She would take an orange to Lucy, then carry the rest down to the kitchen. Maybe somebody there could unravel the mystery.

Matt was with his mother. "Good morning," he said. "I see you got my oranges."

"*You* left these outside my door?"

"Yes."

Sandi nearly burst out laughing, but the expression on his face stopped her. It was expectation mixed with a kind of awful hope that melted her all the way to her toes.

"Why, that's absolutely lovely," she said.

"You like oranges, then?"

"Yes, I do." Sandi had never known how a smile could tug heartstrings.

"Well, good, then. I'm glad you do."

"As a matter of fact, oranges are my favorite fruit."

That smile again. Lord, why didn't he smile more often? It transformed him.

"There's so much you can do with oranges," she added, and when he said, "I agree," she was as pleased as if he'd proposed something romantic and slightly naughty.

"I used oranges in a book of mine once," Lucy said, and Matt got a funny look on his face. "I used them in the proposal scene."

"This is hardly a proposal," Matt said.

"I should hope not. You haven't even courted her properly yet," Lucy said, and Sandi giggled.

Matt gave them both an aggrieved look. "If you two will excuse me, I have work to do."

Sandi couldn't bear to see him leave thinking he'd failed at romance.

"Matt, wait." She put her oranges on the table and touched his arm. "Thank you. The oranges are a beautiful gift."

"The bowl belongs in the library," he said. "I borrowed it."

Sandi squelched a smile. "All right. I'll put it back."

"No, no. Just keep the oranges in it till you're finished."

Good grief. Matt Coltrane was actually flushed. What in the world was going on?

"Well, thank you again."

She'd already started back toward her art supplies, when he said, "I'll bet you haven't seen the rose garden."

"Only from my window and from the courtyard in the dark."

"I'll show it to you."

"That will be lovely."

"All right, then. Come on."

She glanced at her art supplies, and Lucy made shooing motions with her hand. "Have fun," she said, and Sandi took the arm Matt offered.

He was rather proud of himself. His foray into romance had cheered his mother, and if the smile on Sandi's face was any indication, he hadn't done too badly with her, either. Not that he wanted to impress her, but he certainly didn't want her thinking he was a man of less than sterling talents anywhere he chose to apply them.

For the time being, that would be in the foreign arena of romance.

"I decided you were right," he told Sandi. "About granting Mother her last wish."

"So that's what the oranges were all about."

"Yes." Remembering his recent success, he smiled. "The tour of roses, too. Mother can see the garden from her window, and if my guess is right, she'll be all eyes while I romance you in the garden.''

"She *did* seem perkier today."

"If thinking we're falling in love will make her last days happier, then I'll do my part."

Actually, he was glad for a chance to make his mother happy. Now that he thought about it, he'd focused on his work for so long he hadn't paid much attention to anything else.

"And I'll do mine."

"Thank you. You're a generous woman."

"Don't pin any medals on me. Maybe I have ulterior motives."

"You don't."

"How do you know?"

"I'm a lawyer," was all he said. *Never reveal your hand to your opponent.* It was a credo he lived by. The fact was, he'd truly wanted to believe the worst of Sandi Wentworth, but in spite of his best intentions to prove her evil, she'd turned out to be a decent woman.

That should make this faux courtship easier. Or harder. Depending on the viewpoint.

Matt wasn't fixing to explore the latter viewpoint. He'd put on an act to make his mother happy, and when it was all over, he would go about his business as usual.

The rose garden lay just ahead. Out of the corner of his eye he saw a shadow at his mother's window.

"She's watching," he said.

"Good."

"The first rose you see is an old French bourbon, cultivated in 1828. Its perfume is musky and not at all subtle, as you might expect of the French."

"It's magnificent," Sandi replied.

"The yellow rose on the left is sunsprite. Aunt Kitty planted it near the courtyard because of its cinnamon-like fragrance."

"Oh, I love yellow. It's so cheerful, don't you think?"

"Cheerful?"

"Yes, like the sun."

"I suppose."

"Have you ever noticed that you can be blue, and all of a sudden the sun will come out and you start feeling better for no other reason?"

"No. I never noticed. I don't believe in mood swings.... The pink rose is a grandiflora called Tournament of Roses. Its blooms are larger than..."

"Matt..."

"Yes?"

"All this history of the rose garden is really interesting..."

"Good. I'm glad you like it." Matt congratulated himself on his second romantic success of the day.

"I do. But I think your mother is going to be looking for something more."

"It's too early in the make-believe courtship for clenches in the garden."

"Yes, but don't you think we should at least hold hands?"

He could handle that. No problem at all. Matt

reached for her hand and felt gut-punched. Good God, it was a conspiracy. A bunch of female angels must have ganged up on the Almighty and said, "Look, you've got to make women's hands soft and fragile feeling so men will lose their minds."

Well, he wasn't fixing to lose his mind. He would just run his thumb around her palm to check out the size and give her tender knuckles a caress or two in case Lucy was looking, and then he would...

Lose his mind.

And that just from holding her hand. What would happen when he kissed her?

No sense losing sleep over it.

He cupped her face and tipped it up to the sun, and every sane thought flew out of his head. All because of her eyes. And the dewy softness of her skin. And the way her lips parted, pink and damp and delicious-looking.

He leaned over and took a taste. Then another. And another.

Something wonderful and awful and glorious and terrible happened. She was in his arms and he was holding her so close he could feel her heart beating next to his and he didn't want to quit kissing her. Not ever.

To make matters worse, she was making satisfied little cat's-in-the-cream sounds. Spurred like a stallion in the Kentucky Derby, he deepened the kiss, plunged his tongue inside her mouth and nearly crossed the finish line.

Alarmed, Matt broke the kiss and stepped back.

Sandi glowed. That's the only way he could describe the way she looked. It was terrible and awful and absolutely the most amazing thing that had ever happened to Matthew Coltrane. *Nobody* had ever glowed because of him.

He silently congratulated himself on having the foresight to read one of his mother's books. Tonight he might read another.

"Ohhh," Sandi said. "That was perfect."

"Yes."

Suspended, they stared at each other and merely breathed. Air had never tasted so sweet.

"It was absolutely the most wonderful kiss—"

"Yes."

She blushed. "For your mother's sake, I mean."

"Of course. Naturally, it was all for her benefit."

"Well, obviously."

"You were right. We have to make our romance look authentic."

"Oh, I agree. Absolutely."

He lifted her fragile hand to his lips and planted a soft kiss there. For his mother's sake.

Sandi sighed in a delightful "ohhhhing" kind of way that warmed Matt in places he hadn't even known were cold.

"I think we should do it again," he said, "in case she wasn't looking the first time."

"Ohhh, yesss!"

She tilted her face to his, and he discovered that kissing her was something he didn't have to train for by reading a book. It came naturally.

The force of his desire shocked him, and he stepped back from her immediately.

There was no need to take their playacting further. No spying eyes would follow them into the bedroom. *Separate* bedrooms. With the connecting door locked.

Matt planned to keep it that way, and so he launched into the rose tour with feverish intent.

"The next rose is in a class called—"

"I have to be going," she said.

"Going?"

"Back inside."

"Oh, back inside." Relief made him weak-kneed.

"Yes. To…to do some sketching. Of your mother. Before…"

"Yes, yes. I understand. We've done enough for today."

"Have we?"

"Well, maybe not for the entire day. Perhaps to-night…"

"Tonight?"

He suddenly had visions of Sandi spread upon his bed. He was speechless. She touched her lips. The extremely soft, infinitely desirable, utterly irresistible lips he'd so recently kissed.

"I see." She smiled. "See you tonight."

He stood with his feet taking root in the garden soil until Sandi was out of sight. Then he sat down in the nearby gazebo and dreamed of tonight.

For the sake of his mother, of course.

In the safety of her bedroom, Sandi leaned against the wall with her hand pressed over her runaway heart. "What have I done?"

The wall was the only thing holding her up. This simply couldn't be happening. Not again. She had to stop thinking that *man* plus *kiss* plus *rapidly beating heart* equals *love*.

"It was all make-believe," she said.

And with that, she held a cool cloth to her flushed face, combed her hair and went to find Lucy.

Lucy sat in a chaise beside the window looking youthful and healthy.

"You look flushed, my dear," she said.

Sandi automatically said, "The sun," then flushed even deeper.

"Ah, yes, the sun." Lucy patted the chaise. "Come, dear, sit by me and tell me if my son's any good at kissing."

"What?"

"I saw you from the window."

Of course she had. Wasn't that the whole point? Sandi realized she could tell Lucy exactly how she felt and get the benefit of advice from a wise woman who was an expert at romance, while at the same time granting Lucy's fondest wish.

"I know my son's a stick-in-the-mud, but it did look to me as if the two of you were *lost* in each other."

"We were. *I* was."

"Matt, in love at last. You don't know how happy that makes me."

"I can't speak for Matt, and I'm confused about my

own feelings. I've never felt anything like that. Ever. But I've been in love so many times, I'm just not sure anymore.''

''Those teenage crushes never amount to much.''

''I've been engaged several times, and each time one of them left I thought I'd be brokenhearted. But I wasn't. Not once. Just miffed and a little ego-bruised.''

''I never would have dreamed...''

Sandi blushed. ''Please don't think I'm loose. Phoebe taught me never to give myself unless I was certain the man would treasure the gift.''

''Ah, yes. Beautiful Phoebe. Everybody loved her.''

''So did I. She was like a mother to me.''

''She was right, you know. And so you thought these men treasured you?''

''No. Not really. Everything always happened so fast.... Oh, but I'm tiring you out with my problems.''

''Nonsense, dear. I'm healthy as a horse... I mean, I *was* healthy as a horse before the heart attack.''

''I'm so sorry.''

''You're one of the good things that has come from this misfortune.''

''I feel the same way about you. I really love you and this fabulous old house—''

''And Matt.''

''I don't know, and I don't know how to tell.''

Lucy got a dreaming look on her face. ''I was in love once,'' she said. ''But I made a terrible mistake. He wanted to wait and I wanted instant gratification and so when Henry Coltrane came along and promised me the moon, I said yes."

Lucy gave Sandi a piercing look. "Don't ever make that mistake, dear. Always follow your heart."

"I'm not sure I know how. I used to believe I was following my heart, but now that I look back, I'm not so sure."

"The heart whispers in our ear, but we often don't hear because the ego is screaming so loudly we mistake the cacophony for wisdom and common sense and rational thinking. Don't ignore your heart whispers, my dear."

"I'll try not to. Are you up to my sketching a bit?"

"Absolutely." Lucy struck a pose, and Sandi squelched her laughter.

"Just be yourself. I'll do a series of sketches, then we'll discuss which one you want me to paint on canvas."

"I want to look young."

"You do."

"And beautiful."

"You are."

"And sexy."

Sandi started laughing and Lucy joined her. That's the way it went all afternoon, sketching and talking and laughing until finally Kitty joined them with a platter of cookies.

"If we're going to have a party, we need food." She winked at Lucy. "Low fat, on account of your heart."

Dolly came in trailing an ostrich-plume boa and

Kitty said, "Good grief, Dolly, you look like you're molting."

"I probably am. Birds deprived of sex start losing their feathers."

"I never heard that," Kitty said, and Lucy told her, "That's because she made it up."

"Don't pay them any mind," Dolly told Sandi. "There're just a couple of old fuddy-duddies."

Lucy said, "If I weren't dying—" and the three women all started laughing again.

Sandi had never seen anything as brave. She'd heard laughter through tears was cathartic, but this was her first time to witness it. She wished she didn't ever have to leave this house and the company of these women…and Matt.

He appeared as suddenly as if she'd thought him up.

"What's going on in here?" Spying cookies, he whisked the platter off the table. "Mother, you know you're not supposed to eat these."

Lucy looked chagrined, and Dolly said, "Party pooper."

"That's right. Party's over. Mother, you should be resting." He turned a fierce look on Kitty and Dolly. "And you two should be ashamed."

"We're not," Dolly said.

"As for you, young lady…" Matt turned his intense scrutiny on Sandi, and she wondered if she should bow, raise her right hand and swear to tell the truth or giggle. "I'm taking you out of here before these three think up any more mischief."

She felt a blooming in her spirit. "Where?" she asked, not that it really mattered. Anywhere would be great as long as it was with him.

"To the lake. We'll go sailing so you can see the sunset."

"That's very romantic, Matt," Lucy said. "I think I wrote a scene like that once in—"

"This is not a scene in one of your books, Mother. We're just going sailing."

Chapter Five

Not that he was any expert on the subject, but Matt believed he could tell a lot about a woman by observing the way she watched a sunset. Sandi didn't merely watch a sunset, she participated in it. Leaning on her elbows, she hung over the edge of the sailboat with her face turned toward the west while the evening sun gilded her gold and pink and vermilion. A hint of a smile played around her lips and every now and then she made a satisfied little sound, as if hummingbirds were trapped in her throat.

"Look at that sky," she said. "Have you ever seen anything so beautiful?"

"No," he said, but he wasn't looking at the sky.

"I wish I could duplicate those colors."

He didn't hear a word Sandi said because he was

lost somewhere between desire and wonder. She turned around and touched him on the shoulder.

"Matt, are you okay?"

She was close and soft and sweet-smelling, and he didn't need any crash courses in romance to guide him. The minute his lips touched hers, she yielded. Heart to heart, they kissed while the sun dropped over the horizon, leaving ribbons of color streaked across the sky and reflected in the water.

When they finally separated, Sandi murmured, "It's getting too dark for your mother to see."

"Of course," he said, not that he'd given his mother a passing thought. In fact, even if she were searching the lake with binoculars, she couldn't see them because he'd sailed around the bend, and a copse of oak and pine and cedar blocked her view. Thankfully, Sandi pretended not to notice.

"Are you hungry?" he asked, and loved the way she stared at him when she said, "Hmm, yes."

"I stopped by the kitchen and Kitty packed us a picnic dinner."

"Oh, good."

"With oranges."

"Delicious."

Matt wondered if she'd read the same romance he'd read.

"Matt, what's in the picnic basket...besides oranges?"

"Let's see..." To his utter amazement, he realized he didn't know. The only thing he'd wanted in that basket was oranges, though he had absolutely no intention of using them for any purpose except what the good Lord intended, as Aunt Kitty would say. Certainly he wasn't about to indulge in the erotic sort of fantasies his mother wrote.

"Do you like surprises, Sandi?"

"Oh, I do."

"Then why don't we open the basket and surprise you?"

Kitty had packed fried chicken, potato salad, rolls and key lime pie, but Matt had eyes only for the oranges...and for Sandi, exclaiming over every item as if she were unloading the crown jewels.

"It doesn't take much to please you, does it?" he said to Sandi, and she simply smiled and shook her head, *no*.

Matt thought that was a wonderful trait in a woman—loving the simple pleasures of life. That's one of the traits he would be looking for if he were looking. Which, of course, he wasn't.

"Oh, look, Kitty even put in a white linen tablecloth."

Sandi shook it out and it billowed on the deck like an invitation for a night of forbidden delights. Fortunately she spread nothing except food on the beckoning cloth, and his sanity partially returned.

It made another quick exit as he listened to Sandi's uninhibited appreciation of the food.

"Mmm, wonderful," she said of the chicken, then, "Oh, delicious," regarding the potato salad. Or perhaps it was the pie. He was too deep in fantasies to know.

"Matt?"

"Yes?"

"Aren't you hungry?"

"Starving."

She gave him a puzzled look. "You haven't touched a thing."

"I was enjoying the view first." He gazed studiously out over the water. "I never get tired of it."

"I can see why."

Nearly caught you, didn't she? his nasty-minded conscience said, but he busied himself scarfing down key lime pie and ignored it.

Suddenly Sandi leaned toward him, and she was in exactly the right place for kissing. If he wanted to.

"You have pie—" her finger touched the side of his mouth "—right there."

"Kiss it off," he said, and she did. He completely forgot his conscience and his faux courtship and his fantasizing.

This was real. So real he could no longer hold back the tide of passion that swept over him. With one arm he raked the food out of the way and with the other he lowered her to the cloth. She reached for his shirt and he reached for hers while the last ribbons of gold faded into a velvet-blue dusk that covered their naked bodies like a benediction.

He reached for an orange, bit out a plug and squeezed the juice over her sweet breasts. So much for his good intentions. Feasting, he never knew when she found the orange and anointed his fingers. Then one by one she savored them.

"You read the same book," he said, and she said, "Yes," then pulled his head back down to her breasts while she made sounds that pierced his rapidly thawing heart.

It had been so long since he'd had a woman. When she arched against him, he drove deep inside and released them both.

"I'm sorry," he said, and she covered his lips with her fingertips.

"Don't," she whispered, then pulled him back to her and said, "Stay."

Cushioned in her soft body, Matt slowly came back to awareness. She was stroking his hair, making those soft murmuring noises that sounded like humming birds in the hayloft of his grandfather's barn. But he was no longer a child and he certainly wasn't in a barn.

He untangled himself with the alacrity of a man suffering the all-too-common disease of *if only*—if only he hadn't suggested a sail at sunset, if only he hadn't packed oranges, if only he hadn't read his mother's book, if only he'd maintained control.

He jerked upright and scrambled for their clothes. "Cover yourself," he said, then turned his back while she did.

"It's okay," she kept saying.

"It is *not* okay. It's unforgivable."

"You can turn around now."

"Are you decent?"

"Yes."

He wanted to die. He'd carelessly robbed her of her

virginity, and still she gazed at him with a forgiving smile and a radiance that terrified him.

It would be just like her to believe she'd fallen in love. After all, she was an artist, and weren't they known for their romanticism, their loose grasp of the facts, their lead-with-your-heart approach to life?

"God, why didn't you tell me you were a virgin?"

"You never asked."

He'd never expected to need to know. "You should have told me." The best defense is a strong offense.

"There's no need to growl."

"I'm not growling."

"Yes, you are."

"Okay, okay. You're right. Look, I'm sorry, Sandi. If only I had known…"

"Matt." Sandi touched his arm and he jerked back as if he'd been shot. "It really is okay."

"My God, how can you say that? I took your virginity." And in a manner that embarrassed the hell out of him, but he didn't say that. Didn't even want to admit it to himself, let alone her. "How in the hell was I to know that a woman who had been engaged so many times was still a virgin?"

"Phoebe taught me to save myself for someone who would treasure me."

Matt groaned, and she hastened to add, "Don't worry about it."

"How can you say that? I wasn't even wearing protection. I assumed you…"

"I said, don't *worry*. I plan to forget this little incident ever happened."

Little incident, was it? "So do I."

"You don't have to shout."

"I'm not shouting. I'm being firm. You're the one riled."

"I am not *riled.* I'm cold." She wrapped her arms around herself and shivered. "Stress always makes me cold."

"I'm sorry I stressed you."

"Apology accepted. Can we please go home now?"

"Gladly."

He was so mad, he jerked the anchor and it slammed into his boat. It probably did several hundred dollars' worth of damage. *Good.* Served him right for all the damage he'd done tonight.

He took the wheel while Sandi stood huddled at the bow with her back to him. Matt felt like the world's biggest heel. Furthermore, he felt like a fraud.

"The game's over," he said.

"What do you mean?" She turned to face him, and darned if she didn't have tears in her eyes. He wanted to hit something, and hit it hard.

"This foolish pretense stops rights here."

"But your mother..."

"Mother will just have to get over it, that's all."

Sandi glared at him for a full three minutes, gathering steam, no doubt, because when she spoke there were razor blades and nails in her voice.

"We will *not.* We've already started it, and we're not going to back out now."

"The game takes two, and I'm not playing."

"Why?"

"Isn't that obvious?"

"Yes. You're chicken."

"You can't tell me you want to go on after what happened here tonight."

"If you don't stop bellowing at me I'm going to throw something. And I warn you, my aim is good. I played girls' softball in high school. Pitcher."

He'd never seen a woman who could enrage him and inflame him at the same time. God, she looked so delicious standing there with her hands on her hips and her thoroughly kissed breasts pink in the moonlight, he almost lost control again.

"Button your blouse," he said.

"I can't."

"Why not?"

"You tore off the buttons."

So he had. They lay scattered about the deck like tiny pearls of regret.

"All right," he said. "You win."

"I do?"

"Yes, you do. I knew better than to argue with you in the first place."

"Why?"

"There's no way a man can win when he's dealing with a steel magnolia."

"Matt..." She sailed toward him, all pink and soft and glowing, and when she put her hand on his, he nearly came undone. "Thank you. I won't disappoint your mother."

He looked at her, really looked, and his hands tightened on the wheel.

"There are some pins down below," he said. "Go
fasten your blouse."

So, what had happened last night? She couldn't
blame it on the moon. She'd had moonlight dates before. She couldn't blame it on her desire for a child.
She'd wanted a baby for years. Surely, it wasn't love.
If she loved him, she'd know, wouldn't she?

Sex was not all it was cracked up to be. That's what
Sandi thought. And yet she woke up feeling like a
different woman, richer somehow, softer and full of
delicious secrets.

She brushed her teeth and studied herself in the mirror to see if she looked any different. She was a bit
disappointed to discover there was nothing that would
make Lucy say, "I see you've seduced my son."

That's what Sandi had done. Not that she'd meant
to. Still, she'd encouraged him every step of the way.
She hadn't said no.

Suddenly the enormity of what she'd done sank in,
and she sat on the edge of the cold porcelain tub. My
lord, this had never happened with any of her fiancés,
and she'd loved all three of them. Or so she had
thought…. Until she was practically at the church
door, and then the truth sank in. She'd been in love
with the idea of love, not the men. What would she
say when she saw Matt?

She jumped up to practice in front of the mirror.

"Hi, Matt. I enjoyed last night."

That wouldn't do. It sounded like an invitation.

"Oh, hello, Matt. Thanks for the sail."

That was too cold, too nonchalant. She had to think of something that would put him at ease and let him know that nothing had changed.

Liar. Everything's changed.

What if she were pregnant? Too late to worry about that now. What was done was done.

Oh, she wished she could talk to Lucy about what had happened, but that was out of the question. She wished she could talk to Phoebe, but that was impossible. And C.J. would be in class. She would just have to muddle through on her own.

Her heart hammered as she dressed and hurried to the kitchen. The smell of coffee stopped her in the hallway. Sandi closed her eyes and took a deep breath, then pasted a smile on her face and called a cheerful greeting to announce her arrival.

"Good morning, Matt."

"Sorry to disappoint you."

Dolly sat at the table dressed in befeathered splendor, watching TV. When Sandi walked in, she pressed the remote control to turn off an early-morning news report on the president's visit to the Middle East.

"Oh…" Sandi tried to hide her disappointment and probably didn't succeed. She was a terrible actress, always leading with her heart and always telling the truth, no matter what. "You've changed your hair."

"Yes. I was a redhead for the stage role I was playing before Lucy became ill. I got tired of being a redhead and decided to go back to my original blond."

"It's really quite stunning." Sandi meant what she said. "It makes you look about ten years younger."

"Darling, I hope you stay here forever."

"I do, too."

"Good!"

"Oh, I didn't mean that the way it sounded. It's just that this old house is so wonderful. Being here feels like having arms wrapped around me all the time."

"I know. That's why I come here every chance I get. I practically live here." She poured Sandi a cup of coffee, studying her with a shrewdness that someone less observant might have missed. "Here, you look like you need it."

"Yes, I do."

"Anything you want to talk about?"

"Thank you, but I really can't."

Dolly turned her intense scrutiny on Sandi once more. Finally she said, "Always follow your heart."

"That's what Lucy said."

"She's right." Dolly took a long sip of coffee, then cradling the cup in her hands, she got a faraway look in her eyes. "I've always wondered what my life would be like now if I'd listened to my heart instead of reason."

Sandi was shocked. Here was a woman who had it all—a great career, loyal friends, an adoring public, a beautiful adopted daughter. What had she wanted that she didn't have?

"Ms. Wilder..." She seemed not to have heard. "Dolly..." Sandi touched her hand. "Are you all right?"

The woman's laughter was so convincing, Sandi chided herself for presuming that a woman of Dolly

Wilder's fame would need solace from someone she hardly knew.

"I'm *great.*" Dolly glanced at the clock on the wall. "If you want to catch Matt before he leaves, you'd better hurry."

"Matt's leaving?"

"He has a case in Jackson that comes to trial today."

Sandi felt sick all the way to her toes. "Oh...where is he?"

"With Lucy."

Matt was impatient to get on the road before Sandi woke up.

"Mother, I wish you'd change your mind and let me call Jolie and Elizabeth," he said, referring to his sisters. "Or at least call Elizabeth."

"Jolie's goodness-knows-where down in Peru, and Elizabeth's in the midst of her documentary in Wales. There's no need to upset her right in the middle of it, and there's certainly no need for her to rush home. I'm not planning to die anytime soon."

"I know that, Mother. Still, I don't like keeping your condition from them. They'll have my hide when they find out."

"No, they won't. You take care of my business and let me take care of my daughters."

Matt sighed. His mother had always been stubborn, but the heart attack had enhanced the irritating trait. He glanced anxiously at his watch.

"I have to be going. Follow Ben's orders and don't party in here after bedtime."

Lucy looked aggrieved. "Would I do such a thing?"

"Yes." Hearing footsteps in the hall, he grabbed his briefcase. "I'll be back in two days. Three at most."

"Matt, wait. Aren't you going to say goodbye to Sandi?"

"Tell her for me."

"But, Matt…"

He rushed out, leaving his mother still talking, which wasn't like him at all. Nothing he'd done lately was like him. Last night, for instance…

"Matt…"

Sandi was standing at the end of the hallway in shorts and a top no bigger than his handkerchief, looking delicious and irresistible. Looking like the kind of woman who would turn a man into a complete fool.

He lifted his hand in salute, then fled. And just in the nick of time, too. By the time he got to his car he was so wracked by desire he was not fit for decent company.

Embarrassing, that's what it was.

Why had he ever agreed to her little game in the first place? Deception never paid.

Watching Matt leave without so much as a goodbye, Sandi felt like a woman spurned.

She watched until he was out of sight, hoping he would change his mind and rush back at the last minute to say, "Sandi, I've thought of nothing but us since last night, and when I get back we'll take up where we left off." Or words to that effect.

He didn't come back, of course. She entered Lucy's bedroom in time to see Matt's car disappearing down the driveway.

"Good morning, Sandi. Come, sit down and tell me all about last night."

Good grief. How did Lucy know? Had Matt told her?

"Last night?"

"The sail. You and Matt did go sailing, didn't you?"

"Oh, yes, we went sailing."

Flooded with relief, Sandi sat down beside Matt's mother and described the sunset. She didn't leave out a single color.

Dolly and Kitty had gathered in Lucy's room for a late-night emergency meeting. They all sat cross-legged on Lucy's bed eating nachos with cheese dip.

"What are we going to do about Ben?" Lucy asked them.

"Tell us again," Kitty said. "Exactly what did he say when he called?"

"He said Matt had left six messages and he didn't like deceiving him and he couldn't stay off fishing forever."

"What's so bad about that?" Dolly asked. "Judging by the looks of Sandi this morning, I'd say our plan has already worked. She's in love."

"I could have told you that," Kitty said.

"My son's in love?" Lucy was miffed that she hadn't noticed, especially since she was the expert. "How do you know?"

"I put a little something extra in the key lime pie."

"What?" Lucy and Dolly said together.

"Remember that aphrodisiac I put in Professor Timmons's tea?"

Timmons had been the most hated professor at the university, stern and forbidding until the night of the spring fling when Kitty had slipped him a little love potion. He'd chased the librarian till he caught her and after three days of scandal and debauchery, they ended up at the justice of the peace.

"He and Evelyn Larkin honeymooned in Tahiti," Dolly said.

"Matt doesn't like Tahiti," Lucy said. "He'll take Sandi somewhere more civilized."

"What else did Ben say?" Dolly asked.

"None of your business," Lucy said, though of course she knew she would eventually tell them. The women always shared their secrets. She just wanted to draw out the suspense a little longer.

"Kitty, maybe you ought to fix Ben's tea the next time he comes," Dolly said, and Lucy shouted, "Don't you dare."

Chapter Six

Driving home in the middle of the night was a cow-ardly thing to do, but Matt figured he would simply add that to his list of sins. *Coward, liar, virgin spoiler.*

Though it was two in the morning when he arrived and chance encounters were unlikely, he sneaked into his own house like a thief. When he got to the east wing he even took off his shoes in case Sandi was a light sleeper.

That thought led him down an erotic pathway that had him tossing and turning till dawn. When his alarm clock went off, he felt as if he'd been run over by a lumber rig and left on the road to die.

He hastened to the kitchen with the idea of grabbing his coffee and a muffin before anybody would be there. Feeling surly and out of sorts, he rounded the corner and who should he see except the one person in the world he wanted to avoid.

"Good morning."

It was just his bad luck that Sandi Wentworth looked as delicious before sunrise as she did at sunset.

"You can stop playing Miss Hospitality. No one's watching."

Her smile vanished, and he felt like a cad. His heart whispered for him to say something nice to make amends, while reason screamed at him to keep her at arm's length.

"I know," she said. "I was just trying to be nice."

"Don't waste it on me."

Sandi turned her back on him but not before he saw the hint of tears. Silence screamed around them while Matt poured his coffee and Sandi poured orange juice. When she turned around she was smiling.

"I'm planning to watch the sunrise in the rose garden. Would you like to join me?"

"I don't think Mother will be up this early. And quite frankly, I'm not up to any *performances* today."

"Oh…" Eyes wide, lips parted, Sandi looked like a wounded child.

Matt despised what he had done. "I just thought we could try to be friends."

He put his cup on the table without slamming it down, which was a major achievement considering the raw state of his nerves.

"I said I'd go along with your charade, and I plan to do exactly that. Don't ask for anything more and don't expect it."

She drew herself up and looked six feet tall, although he knew that she was no more than five-six.

"You are the coldest, hardest-hearted man I've ever known."

"Your assessment is correct."

Sandi grabbed her juice and fled while Matt sat at the kitchen table swamped by loneliness and regret. He felt like a man with a gaping hole where his heart ought to be. He felt like the sole survivor of a nuclear winter.

"Pull yourself together," he said.

"Talking to yourself?" It was Aunt Kitty, looking concerned.

"It's a bad habit I've picked up lately."

"Matt..." She sat down at the table and reached for his hand. "You're not like your father."

A memory he'd tried to bury suddenly surfaced. The summer of his thirteenth year, he'd wanted to plan a surprise birthday party for his mother. He'd saved enough money from his paper route to buy balloons and order a fancy cake, then he'd biked down to his father's office to tell him the plans.

It was after five and the receptionist had gone, so Matt made his way back to his daddy's office. As he passed by the examining room he heard sounds. Pushing open the door, he discovered Henry Coltrane *examining* Mrs. Wexford Quentin. Neither of them wore a stitch of clothes.

Matt bolted, and Henry ran after him, calling, "Wait, son, wait."

"This means nothing," Henry told him. "I love

your mother. If you tell her, you'll destroy her and tear the family apart. You don't want to do that, now, do you, son?''

That had been Matt's initiation into manhood, the summer of his thirteenth year when he promised to keep his father's awful secret.

Even now the memory of what he'd done made Matt sick.

''How did you know?'' he asked his aunt.

''I was your father's nurse, Matt. Nothing escaped me.''

''But you never told Mother?''

''I didn't have to. Lucy knew.''

''I've spent all these years protecting her from a truth she knew all along?''

''Yes.''

''Does Ben know?''

''Yes.''

''Probably everybody in Shady Grove knows.''

''No, I don't think so. Ben would never tell, and the Foxes know how to keep a secret.''

His mother would have told the other Foxes. That sisterhood of women told each other everything. And yet, all these years Lucille O'Banyon Coltrane had lived as if life were a wonderful gift. Her exuberant spirit fooled Matt into believing his mother was on a cosmic carousel ride she enjoyed to the hilt.

''I probably should have talked to you years ago,'' Aunt Kitty added. ''That summer you became such a solemn, serious child. I suspected you had found out.''

"Why now?"

"Because I see you passing up opportunity after opportunity with good, intelligent women...like Sandi."

Matt gripped his coffee cup as if it would anchor him to sanity. The careful world he'd constructed lay in shambles at his feet. The truth he'd believed for so many years was no longer valid.

And yet he was the same coldhearted man he'd always been, wasn't he? He could offer Sandi Wentworth nothing.

Except an apology.

Matt pushed away from the table and kissed his aunt on the cheek.

"Where are you going?"

"To the garden," he said.

Sandi saw Matt coming and ducked out of sight. She had no intention of repeating that sorry performance in the kitchen. She'd said awful things to him, hateful things that made her ashamed.

Besides, she didn't want him to see her crying.

"Sandi? Where are you?"

She wasn't planning to answer, but when she peered around the climbing rose and saw his face, she couldn't help herself.

"Over here. In the gazebo."

He stood in the opening framed by Don Juan roses and looked as uncertain as a little boy who has admitted stealing cookies. Sandi melted.

"The sunrise was beautiful," she said.

"I'm glad." He toyed with a red rose. "I'll leave if you want me to."

"No. Please stay."

"I don't deserve your mercy. I'm a total fool."

"Oh, no. Sometimes you're quite charming."

"Sandi, do you mind if I sit down?"

"No. Please do sit down." She attempted a smile that she hoped fooled him. "After all, it's your gazebo."

He sat on the adjacent side, and Sandi felt a quick stab of disappointment.

"I came to apologize," he said.

"I'm the one who should apologize. I said hateful things to you, and—"

"Sandi, don't." He scooted around and touched a finger to her lips. "Shh. I don't give in to noble instincts very often. Please, let me finish."

"Okay."

"I'm sorry I made you cry. It was not my intention and certainly not my desire."

Her cheeks flushed at his choice of words while memories of being in his arms on the sailboat washed over her.

"Sandi, can you forgive me?"

"I forgive you, Matt."

"Thank you."

He captured her hand then turned it palm up and planted a soft kiss that made Sandi wish for more. Glancing toward Lucy's window, she saw nothing except closed curtains.

"Your mother's not watching."

"I know."

Suspended in their cocoon of grace, they sat hand in hand while the stillness built into a storm of desire that caught them both unaware.

Matt suddenly bolted out of his seat as if firecrackers had gone off in his pants. "I have to be going."

She didn't say, "Please stay." She didn't dare.

Sandi didn't see Matt the rest of the day, which was probably a good thing. Her emotions were so jumbled she didn't know what to say to him, what to do around him.

Though she was busy most of the day sketching Lucy, she kept an eye out for him, just in case. Late in the afternoon the sun vanished into an angry-looking bank of storm clouds, and by evening thunder and lightning ripped the sky.

Sandi glanced anxiously out the window. "It looks like a tornado brewing."

"You're not afraid, are you, Sandi?" Lucy said.

"I have to confess, storms terrify me. My daddy was killed in a tornado."

"Oh, my dear, I'm so sorry. How awful that must have been for you and your mother."

Sandi and her mother had cried for weeks. Meredith's grief ended abruptly when Rafe Perkins crashed into the back of their car and into their lives. By the time Sandi emerged from her grief, Meredith had discarded Rafe in favor of a leather-maker she'd found on her first-anniversary trip to Mexico. He doted on the four-year-old Sandi, and that was his undoing. Her mother promptly ditched him and found Maxwell Garber, who doted on only two things: Meredith and the Wentworth money.

Fortunately, Sandi's father had secured money for his daughter in a trust that neither Meredith nor Maxwell could touch. Maxwell lasted no longer than it took for him to find out the truth. Before Sandi could breathe a sigh of relief at his departure, Meredith Wentworth Perkins Santiago Garber had added Martin to her name.

Sandi lost count after that because she was too old for Meredith to play the young mother of a cute little child. Bundled off to Mississippi like damaged goods so her mother could live a high-flying life in Paris, she might have died of soul starvation if it hadn't been for C.J. and her parents.

Lucy's voice brought her out of her reverie. "Sandi? Are you all right?"

"Yes, I'm fine, thank you."

"Don't worry about the tornado, dear. This house is engineered to withstand the worst storms Mississippi can produce. If you need anything, Matt is right next door."

"Thanks, I'll remember that."

"Well, then, you have a good evening, my dear."

Sandi kissed Lucy's cheek. "You, too. Get some rest. I'll see you in the morning."

She stored her art supplies then grabbed a sandwich in the kitchen and went to find a good book. Lightning lit the windows of the library and Sandi flinched. She settled into a chair and tried to read, but a boom of thunder sent her racing to the safety of her bedroom, a smaller, cozier space without the huge banks of windows to showcase the storm.

"The terror is all in my mind," she told herself. "The storm can't touch me."

She put on her nightgown, climbed into the middle of the wonderful old bed and finally lost herself in the book. It was one of Lucy's, *Flames of Love.*

While the storm gathered force outside, Sandi found herself laughing and crying and wishing she were the heroine Marguerite, who found a hero to love her forever.

Suddenly the house shook with thunder and her room lit up with streaks of lightning that looked like fire. Sandi bolted out of bed and through the connecting door.

Cozy in their bed socks, the women were lined up on Lucy's king-size bed watching television. Out of the blue, Kitty said to Lucy, "You've got to talk to Matt."

"Shh," Lucy said. "This is the good part."

"Lucy, you can't avoid the truth forever."

"Yes, you can," Dolly said, then turned up the TV volume.

Kitty would not be deterred. "Matt knows about Henry. He kept the secret from you all these years, and it's eating him alive. The two of you need to clear the air. And while you're at it, you need to tell him you're not dying."

Dolly turned to Lucy and said, "She's probably right about that, Lucy. Matt's already in love with Sandi. All we're doing with this charade is muddying the waters."

Lucy looked chagrined. "I can't."

"Why not? You've got more guts than that, Lucille Coltrane." Kitty rarely got riled, but when she did she could be a bulldog.

"Josh is coming tomorrow to make sure my soul is right with God."

Kitty took umbrage. "He didn't peep it to me." Her only child was fixing to descend on O'Banyon Manor and hadn't even told her.

"Imagine, the Reverend Josh O'Banyon walking into our little den of deceit," Dolly said, and started laughing.

Her two friends looked at her as if she'd lost her mind, then joined in. They laughed so hard they had to clutch each other to keep from falling off the bed.

Finally Lucy reached for tissue and passed it around. "What have we done now?"

"We've done worse," Dolly said.

Her two friends grabbed her hands and held on tight.

The fragrance of gardenia penetrated his sleep, and for a moment Matt thought he was in the courtyard. He burrowed deeper into his pillow and tried to find escape once more in deep sleep, but it eluded him. Thinking a change of position would help, he rolled over to his left side…right into a huddled lump of perfumed softness.

"I didn't mean to wake you," she said.

"Sandi?" He moved back across his bed with the alacrity of a man running from stinging bees. "What are you doing in my bed?"

"I'm scared of the storm."

He was thinking that was the oldest ploy in the book and was fixing to revise his opinion of her.

Then she added, "My daddy died in a tornado when I was three."

"Come here."

She moved into his arms and he held her tight. Sighing, she snuggled closer and he buried his face in her fragrant hair and it seemed they had always been this way.

"This feels so good," she whispered, and he said, "Yes."

Because it did. Because it was the middle of the night when guards were down. And because being by yourself in a bed, or even being with the wrong person in a bed, was the loneliest feeling in the world.

The elements renewed their fury and Sandi muffled her scream against his chest. He could feel the tremors in her body, feel her terror.

"It's okay." He caressed her back in long, slow strokes. "It's all right. I'm here."

She turned her face up to his and in the brilliant flash of lightning that bounced around the room he could see her eyes bright with tears.

He cupped her face and kissed her with all the tenderness a kiss of comfort is meant to convey. Sighing, she fell into the kiss. They both did, and suddenly it was not comfort they sought, but something more.

Her gown was thin and silky, her body soft and enticing. It felt like heaven. It felt like redemption.

He ran his hands down the long length of silk, then back up, skimming bare skin, reveling in sweet soft flesh.

"Sandi?"

"Yes," she whispered.

"Wait here." He slipped from the bed, determined to be safe this time. When he returned, he kissed her eyes, her lips, the tender skin behind her earlobe. And when his lips moved over her throat then down to her breasts, she caught his hair and pulled him to her, moaning.

His tongue wet the silk, teased the taut nipple beneath. Sliding his hand underneath her gown he found her hot, wet core while he suckled her through the thin fabric of her gown. It was a potent mix.

He stripped aside her gown and it pooled on the floor while he explored her storm-lit body. His tongue branded her belly, the tender skin of her inner thighs. Burying his face in her nest of curls he inhaled the musky, ready scent of her, delved his tongue inside to taste, explored deeply till he found the spot that made her arch upward, speared by pleasure.

This, he thought, *this is the way it should be.*

"There," she whispered. "Right there. Don't move."

She held his head fast while he took her over the

edge again and again until she was begging, "Please, please, please," and he was mindless with desire.

As he lifted over her, he saw how beautiful she was, golden hair spread across the pillow, eyes bright with passion, lips parted and slightly swollen from their kisses.

Covering her mouth with his, he slid into her, slid so deep her eyes widened. With a cry of pure pleasure, she pulled him close and held him there while spasm after spasm shook her.

He loved the sounds she made, loved the way she expressed her pleasure, loved that he was the cause.

Her breath came out on a long sigh. "Ohhh, that was wonderful."

"There's more."

"More?"

"Much, much more," he said, then took up a rhythm that she matched perfectly, as if they'd always danced this erotic, primal dance, as if they'd been fashioned especially for each other, programmed so that only the two of them together matched.

With Sandi in his arms Matt was insatiable, unflappable, invincible.

The pace of their lovemaking escalated till it matched the fury of the storm outside. Taking Sandi with him, Matt rolled to his back and watched with a combination of tenderness mixed with awe while she discovered how a woman in charge can own the world.

Head thrown back, hands clenched with his, body racked by spasms, she cried out his name over and over.

Sweat-slick, nerves vibrating like too-tight piano wires, Matt rolled her onto her back and drove into her with a wild abandon that would scare him if he thought about it. But he was beyond thought, beyond reason, almost beyond control.

Her fingernails scored his back while she moaned, "Oh, yes. Yes, yes, yes."

Explosives detonated in him. The dam burst and the river rushed free. She arched high again him, screaming her pleasure, then they both crash-landed on the damp, sweat-tangled sheets.

She caressed his back while he brushed her hair back from her love-lit face.

"Don't move," she whispered.

"All right."

"Stay right there."

"Okay."

He shifted so his chest wouldn't crush her, and she sighed once, softly, then closed her eyes and fell into sweet, peaceful sleep.

Matt watched her until he was certain she wouldn't wake up, then he gently rolled to his side, wrapped her close and held on while wonder filled his soul.

He'd kept the storm at bay for her. He'd erased her fright and eased the terrors of her past.

He felt redeemed.

His redemption was short-lived, however. When he woke up and felt Sandi curled against him, he was racked with guilt. Every detail of their lovemaking was seared into his mind. The thing that wasn't quite so clear was his motive.

Just how much of the previous night's activities had been for Sandi's benefit and how much for his? Sure, he'd made her forget her fear, but hadn't a small part of him wanted to erase his sorry performance on the boat?

Heck, a big part of him had. Male ego. That's what he had.

He looked at the sleeping woman, and desire rose, urgent and painful. How easy it would be to rouse her with a kiss, bury himself in her soft, slick folds and forget everything except satisfying the hunger that clawed at him.

What kind of cad was he turning into?

His father.

Careful not to wake her, Matt eased out of bed, dressed quietly then sat in the wingback chair near the window watching her. She came awake slowly, stretching and yawning. The sheet slid away and he could see how the tender skin around her nipples was still rosy from his attentions, how they stood erect the minute she became aware of his gaze.

"Matt?"

Her eyes glowed softly and her lips were still love-bruised. He wanted nothing more than to shut out the rest of the world, climb back into bed and make love until they were both mindless and sated.

"Good," he said. "You're awake."

With the soft smile of woman well loved, she pulled

the sheet over her breasts. "Last night was wonderful. I never knew it could be like that."

"I'm glad I could take your mind off the storm."

"Oh, you did more than that. Much, much more."

"Sandi." He couldn't sit still, not while she was sitting in his bed naked and desirable and love-struck. "A man can make love with a woman for many reasons. I wanted to help you through your fright."

"Oh, didn't you like it?"

Her artless question nearly unhinged him. "Yes." He raked his hand over his beard stubble and through his hair. "It was enjoyable." *Coward.* "But I don't want you to mistake what happened here. Sex does not equal love and marriage and babies."

"You don't like babies?"

"Well, yes, I love babies, but—"

"I'd like four or five. Maybe six."

"You want six children?"

"Yes. I think large families are so wonderful."

"I do, too, when they belong to someone else."

"Oh."

Matt felt like Ebenezer Scrooge. "Look, Sandi. The bottom line is you and I are acting out a role for Mother's benefit, and we've gotten carried away a couple of times and—"

"Of course." Throwing back the sheets, she arose from the bed, a naked Venus, goddess of everything her lovely green eyes surveyed, cool and completely in control.

Without bothering to cover herself with that little drive-a-man-crazy gown she'd been wearing, she strolled across the rug and patted his face as if he were a wayward and rather backward child.

"Did you think I was talking about *our* children, Matt?"

"You certainly gave that impression."

"You've been working too hard and worrying too much. Why don't you take the day off and have some more *fun?* Don't you worry about me. I'll sit with your mother awhile, sketch a little if she's up to it. Then I thought I might go into Shady Grove, see what sort of *fun* I can find."

Matt pictured her strolling through the streets of the small southern town, an exotic flower among bitter-weeds. The local good old boys would be panting after her like bird dogs after a fox.

"Maybe I should go with you, show you around."

"Don't be silly. I've trekked all over the world alone."

"And collected a fiancé in every port."

Cocking her head to one side as she considered that option, she said, "That is a thought. I'll tell you one thing, though. When I pick a father for my children, it will be a man with a heart."

They glared at each other like adversaries in a Roman arena. Matt was so confused he didn't know whether he was the gladiator or the lion.

Chapter Seven

Avoiding the kitchen altogether, Matt stayed in his mother's office going through the morning mail, and when he finished that, he started sharpening pencils and untangling paper clips. Anything to avoid running into Sandi.

Time crept by on turtle feet. He felt ridiculous hiding out like this. Disgusted, he threw the paper clips back into his mother's desk drawer and strode off to her bedroom. He wasn't about to become a captive in his own house.

He would show Sandi Wentworth that he was a man to be reckoned with, a man who said what he meant and meant what he said. He would tell her in no uncertain terms that there would be no repeat performances of last night, that he'd felt nothing whatsoever except...

"Hi, Matt." Sandi's smile dazzled him, made him forget everything except the way she lit up a whole room. "I was just asking your mother where a girl goes in Shady Grove when she wants to frolic?"

"Frolic?"

"Yes, frolic. You know. Have some fun." He felt like a man who'd had the wind knocked out of him. "I'm off now. Bye." She waggled two fingers at him. "See you later."

Flattened, that's how he felt. Like a man who'd just been run over by a steamroller.

She was the most maddening woman he'd ever met.

"What did you tell her, Mother?"

"I suggested she check out Ray's Pool Hall."

"The *pool* hall?"

"Ray serves the best barbecue in Shady Grove."

"It's full of jocks on the make."

"What's the matter, Matt? Can't you stand a little competition?"

"Good God, Mother. Why didn't you just tell her to stand on the street naked with a sign around her neck?"

"Why, Matt, I do believe you're jealous."

He was fixing to issue a hot denial, when he remembered the damnable charade. Why had he ever agreed? Lord, he needed a break.

"Bye, Mother. See you tonight."

"Where are you going?"

"Into town. I have some things to take care of."

"You're going like that?"

"What do you mean, like that?"

"You haven't shaved."

The beard stubble was all Sandi's fault.

"I'll do it later." Every minute he lost was simply more time for Sandi to get into trouble.

"Matt, is something wrong?"

"Wrong? What would be wrong?"

"You look like you didn't sleep a wink."

"Insomnia," he said, then left quickly before his mother could pry further.

Spurred by half-baked plans and panic, he hurried to his room, grabbed his cordless razor and tore off to Shady Grove. He didn't have a minute to lose.

Shaving with one hand and driving with the other, he tried to firm up his plan, tried to figure out exactly what he would say and do when he found Sandi.

Fortunately, downtown Shady Grove occupied only six square city blocks, so spotting her car was a cinch. She'd gone straight to the pool hall.

"Hell hath no fury like a woman scorned," he said.

Several car horns honked at him. One man even rolled down his window and yelled, "The light's green, you fool."

Sandi Wentworth had him so turned around he was stopping on green to paraphrase poetry. He shot past the pool hall and had to double back. Then he found a parking space and sat in hundred-degree heat with his windows rolled up while he tried to come up with a strategy.

He made his living coming up with winning strategies, and yet not a single idea occurred to him. Finally, Matt just left the car and went into the pool hall.

Though the place was dim even in daytime, he had no trouble spotting Sandi. All he had to do was follow the crowd of admirers. They stood in front of her booth like linebackers guarding the goal.

Matt had never seen a shiftier, sleazier lot of men. He'd arrived in the nick of time. As he stormed to the rescue, he heard them vying for a seat at her corner booth.

"Aw, come on, sugar, let me sit with you."

"Have a heart, beautiful."

"Give a working guy a break, sweetheart."

Matt elbowed his way through, and none too politely, either. "The lady's with me." Sandi opened her mouth to protest, so he slid into her booth and kissed her. Hard.

She came up sputtering, and he had to do it all over again. The fragment of his mind still conscious noticed the men slinking off, one by one.

This time he didn't give her a chance to sputter. He kissed her until he felt her body go slack and her mouth go soft. Her hand stole around his neck, and she made the most delicious murmuring noises he'd ever heard.

If he hadn't been in a public place there's no telling what he might have done. Saved, he broke off the kiss and said, "Let's get out of here."

"I'm hungry."

"So am I," he said, not thinking, not doing anything except *wanting*.

"You'll have to order your own plate. Lucy says the barbecue is divine, and I'm too ravenous to share."

She gave him that glowing, welcoming smile and he'd have eaten the whole pig if she'd asked.

"Fine. We'll eat barbecue." He called the waitress and ordered ribs.

"I'm glad you could join me, Matt. I do want us to be friends."

He could see her romantic wheels turning. First they would chat in cozy corners, get comfortable with each other till their ill-fated encounters faded, then before you knew it, he would be right back where he didn't want to be. Between the sheets while visions of love and commitment danced in her head.

"I came here to rescue you, Sandi. That's all."

"Oh." She fell silent while the waitress put their food on the table. Enough for a small army. He hadn't eaten a bite of breakfast, and sex always made him hungry. Suddenly Matt realized he was starving.

He dug in and it was a while before he noticed her full plate.

"You're not eating."

"I'm not hungry."

"A few minutes ago you were starving."

"I've lost my appetite."

He shoved his plate aside. "Fine, then, we'll leave."

"Go ahead. I'm staying."

"You're not staying here by yourself."

"Oh, yes, I am."

"Dammit, Sandi."

"Getting mad will get you nowhere. I don't like surly men."

Matt ran his hands through his hair, an untidy habit he'd picked up since he met Sandi Wentworth. "You think you can take care of yourself with that bunch of Neanderthals?"

"I don't need you to take care of me."

"Somebody has to do it."

"Ha!" She stood up out of the booth and marched off with her chin up and her back stiff. One of the Neanderthals jumped up to intercept her, but she withered him with one look.

Take that, you overgrown playboy. Matt gloated over his victory for all of ten seconds, then he realized that all he'd done was drive Sandi out of the pool hall. There were plenty of other places in Shady Grove where a woman looking for trouble could go.

He sighed. There was no use trying to stop a woman bent on mischief. He was too old and too tired to follow her all over town, putting out fires.

And he couldn't go back to O'Banyon Manor. His mother would ask too many questions.

In the end, Matt took a hotel room, closed the blinds and fell into bed. He was asleep before his head hit the pillow.

The kitchen floor was cold on her bare feet, but Lucy didn't care. She was starving to death. She licked the crumbs off her fingers and had reached for her third piece of fried chicken when Kitty burst through the door swinging a baseball bat.

Lucy dropped her chicken leg on the floor. "Good grief, put that thing down. You scared me to death."

"I scared *you!* I thought we had a burglar in the kitchen."

"What's all the commotion?" Dolly was wearing so much beauty cream they could see nothing but her eyes.

"Lucy's in the chicken."

"You would be, too, if you'd had nothing but broth and weak tea for days."

"I have no sympathy." Kitty grabbed a piece of chicken for herself. "You should have already told Matt the truth."

"That would spoil everything. I think my son's in love, but he doesn't know it yet. We need a few more days."

"I agree with Lucy." Dolly bypassed the chicken in favor of chocolate cake. "If she tells Matt she's not dying, he'll be so mad he'll leave and then everything we've planned for will go down the drain."

When he got home, Matt pulled off his shoes so he wouldn't wake anybody.

There were no lights underneath Sandi's bedroom door, but he paused anyway. For what he didn't know. She was obviously asleep…in her bed…in the fetching little gown.

He stifled a groan and tiptoed toward his room. Suddenly a door down the hall swung open and there stood his cousin, Josh.

"You finally made it," Josh said. "I never expected to see you tomcatting around here."

"Shh." Matt motioned toward Sandi's door, then

joined his cousin. Open suitcases exploded all over the room. "You've come to stay a while?"

"Two or three days."

Matt laughed. "I see you still pack light."

"Yeah, well, you never know what you might need."

"I'm glad to see you, and I know Mother will be. I can hardly believe she's dying."

"She's not."

"What did you say?"

"I overheard them in the kitchen earlier. She's faking it in order to do a little matchmaking."

"Are you sure?"

"Positive. Otherwise I would never have told you."

Matt had to sit down. Rage warred with relief. "How could my mother have put me through this?"

"Sometimes people do the wrong thing for the right reasons. I'm sure she did it out of love."

"When I finish with her, she'll wish she'd never done it at all."

"Wait a minute, Matt. It's after midnight."

"What better time to catch my opponent off guard?"

"What do you plan to do?"

"Wring a confession out of her. I'm good at that. I'll teach her not to meddle."

"Now, *there's* a good idea. Why don't we teach them a lesson?"

"What did you have in mind, Josh?"

Chapter Eight

Sandi was just emerging from her bath when she heard a knock on the connecting door.

"Sandi, it's Matt."

Well, of course, she knew who it was. Who else would be in his bedroom with the magnificent bed that she couldn't get out of her head no matter how hard she tried? Every time she shut her eyes she saw herself wrapped in his arms in the middle of that beautiful bed just right for conceiving children.

Actually, she didn't even have to shut her eyes. She could be doing an ordinary task like brushing her hair or putting on her shoes, and all of a sudden she'd remember that night and just stand there holding her shoe or her brush, paralyzed.

"Sandi, are you in there?"

"Yes, I'm here."

"I have something very important to discuss with you. May I come in?"

What could be so urgent he couldn't wait until she'd left her bedroom? Or maybe that was the whole point. Maybe he *wanted* to be alone with her in her bedroom.

All sorts of visions came to mind, and every one of them delicious.

"Hmm," she murmured.

"Sandi? Is everything all right in there?"

Everything except her mind. She was losing it. What other reason did she have for mooning over a man who made no bones about his feelings? She wasn't Matthew Coltrane's kind of woman. That was all. The sooner she got that through her head, the better off she would be. The better off they would all be.

"Yes." She unlocked the connecting door and peered around. "Give me a minute. I just got out of the bath."

"Certainly. Take your time."

She vanished behind the closed door and Matt stood in his bedroom shell-shocked. All he could think about was the way she'd looked with little beads of water on her naked shoulder. He'd wanted to lick every drop off, wanted it so badly he had to cram his hands in his pockets to keep from grabbing her.

When she opened her door he had to dally a minute to get himself under control.

"You're sure you don't mind if I come in?"

"Not at all." She swung the door wider. "Excuse the mess. I haven't made the bed yet."

Tangled sheets, still sweet-smelling from where she'd slept. Silk gown, carelessly tossed aside. Strappy high heels kicked off last night. Red. Sexy.

Matt sat down and twisted sideways so she wouldn't see his condition. She sat down opposite him, her robe gaped open, long bare legs crossed, one swinging. He wished she had put on some clothes. But he didn't mention it, didn't want her to know he noticed.

It was a good thing they were going to break up. They would both be saved further embarrassment.

"The reason I wanted to see you this early is that I found out Mother's not dying."

"That's wonderful. I'm so thrilled. I can't wait to see her. Did the doctor misdiagnose her?"

"No. She never was dying. She made it all up in order to do some matchmaking."

"Oh, that's…" Sandi put her hand over her mouth and her shoulders started shaking. For a minute he thought she was crying. Then a peal of laughter escaped.

"I fail to see the humor."

"I'm…" Clapping her hand over her mouth, she tried to stop the laughter, but it exploded, doubling her over. When she came back up for air, tears of mirth streamed down her cheeks. "I'm sorry. I don't mean to make light of this, but just think about it."

"That's all I've been doing all night. I've come up with a plan that I hope meets your approval."

"You sound so serious and…lawyerly."

"That's what I am. Serious and lawyerly. Mother was so busy scheming she forgot that little detail."

"I'm sure she meant well."

"My cousin Josh believes the same thing. He overheard mother with Aunt Kitty and Aunt Dolly."

"Your cousin is here?"

"Yes. He's a preacher so maybe he's right about her meaning well. Still, I think she needs to be taught not to meddle, and that's where you come in…if you agree."

"Well, of course." She would agree to anything that would keep her at O'Banyon Manor. She tried to look helpful but not too eager, cooperative but not too easy, and all the while, her insides were doing exuberant cartwheels. *I'm staying, I'm staying.*

"She threw us together hoping for romance, and we're going to show her disaster."

"Disaster?"

"Yes, we'll break up in a noisy, uncivilized manner that will make Mother wish she'd never heard of romance."

"Isn't that out of character?"

"For me, you mean?"

"Well…I suppose I did. Nobody is surprised at what artists do or say."

"Falling in love is out of character for me, so nothing should come as a surprise." Too late Matt realized his slip of the tongue. If he corrected his statement and said, "pretending to fall in love," that would make his earlier confession even more noticeable.

All he could do was hope Sandi didn't mention it.

"When do we start?" she said.

"Today. After breakfast you go into Mother's room

as usual, and when I come in we'll start a terrible argument. I can't wait to see Mother's face.''

"Oh, your poor mother. I don't want to really upset her.''

"Don't waste your sympathy on my mother. She's fixing to get a dose of her own medicine.''

"Who starts the argument?''

"I'll start, you just play along.''

"What will we argue about?''

"I'll think of something.''

Sandi dressed quickly, thinking she would see Matt at breakfast and they would eat together in a friendly manner befitting coconspirators, but he wasn't there. She lingered, hoping, but he didn't come.

Grabbing her paints, she headed to his mother's room. Lucy was not alone.

"Sandi, come in. I want you to meet my nephew, Josh.''

A tall dark-haired man with the most amazing blue eyes smiled at her.

"You're even more beautiful than Aunt Lucy told me.'' He nodded toward the sketches lying on her worktable beside the window. "You're a good artist, too.''

"And you're a preacher.''

She hadn't meant to say that, but how in the world could she and Matt fight in front of a preacher, cousin or no cousin?

"Guilty.''

He had a winning smile. She'd bet half the women

in his parish fancied themselves in love. That's probably what she would be doing, too, if it weren't for Matt. Not that she fancied herself in love, heaven forbid. She'd promised C.J. that the next time she fell for somebody he would love her right back, and Matt Coltrane certainly didn't do that. He merely tolerated her.

And now he needed her. As much as she hated the idea of doing something that might make Lucy uncomfortable, she owed Matt. After all, she'd been the one who suggested they pretend to fall in love.

"Guilty of what?" Matt entered the room and Sandi could see nothing else. "Responding to Sandi's flirtations?"

"What?"

"You heard what I said. You were down at the pool hall yesterday flirting with every man there."

"I was *not*."

Sandi didn't have to pretend rage. For a make-believe argument, this felt real. Here Matt was carrying on like a jealous lover. She glanced uneasily at Josh, and he winked.

Was he in on it? Matt hadn't said.

"I *saw* you, remember."

"I was eating barbecue."

"With five jocks standing around salivating?"

"Oh my goodness," Lucy said. "Matt, what's gotten into you? I think you should apologize immediately."

"If anybody should apologize, it's Sandi. Men don't swarm around like bees after honey without some sort of provocation."

"You've picked a beautiful woman, Matt. That's all."

"Mother, stay out of this."

Sandi wanted to slap him. "Don't talk to your mother that way."

Matt turned toward his cousin. "Help me out anytime, Josh. It's a conspiracy of women."

Hands on her hips, Sandi marched over and shook her finger in his face. "You're mean, and I won't have it."

"Careful, Sandi. You're about to let your bulldog mouth overload your bird-dog bite."

"And just what are you going to do about it, Matt Coltrane?"

"I know one thing I'm going to do. I'm going to see that you stay away from pool halls."

"And just how do you propose to do that?"

"Tying you up in bed comes to mind."

His eyes smoldered when he looked at her, and all she could think of was making love in a thunderstorm.

"Oh…" She put her hands to her mouth and Lucy came up off the pillows.

"Now, Matt, you stop this nonsense this instant. Take Sandi somewhere private and make up."

Visions of making up with Matt turned Sandi's cheeks pink.

"I have a better idea, Mother. I'll leave her here. While Josh is preparing you for the great beyond, he can lecture Sandi about the wages of sin."

"I think I'm going to be sick." Putting her hand over her forehead, Lucy swooned onto her pillows.

"Matt… Sandi…" She held out her hands. "Don't leave me."

"Well, of course we won't." Pierced by guilt, Sandi sat on the bed and patted Lucy's hand. "I'm so sorry, Lucy. I didn't want you to hear that."

She was sincere. She *hadn't* wanted Lucy to hear an argument between them. What she'd wanted, what she could never admit, especially to Matt, was that he come to her and say, "Look, I've fallen in love with you for real, so we can stop all these shenanigans and everybody can be happy."

She sighed. Why couldn't life have happy endings just like Lucy's romance novels?

"You're sweet." Lucy cupped Sandi's cheek. "Isn't she sweet, Matt?"

"Selectively."

"What is that supposed to mean?" Sandi had thought the bogus fight was over. She was going to have a private talk with Matthew Coltrane. Tonight she was going to march into his room and…

Probably die of desire.

Sighing, she stood up. "I think I'll make some tea. We could all use a cup."

"Amen," Josh said, and she knew good and well he wasn't praying.

Matt was relieved to see Sandi go. Fighting with her had been harder than he'd expected. The way she'd flushed and become sparkly-eyed, she looked as if she took every word personally. The last thing he wanted was to hurt her all over again.

Having Josh in the room had made things a little better, but not much. In fact, when he thought about it, this whole ridiculous charade had been Josh's idea. With the perfect clarity that comes with hindsight, Matt realized he should have followed his instincts. He should have simply confronted Lucy and ended the whole thing.

Nice and clean and easy.

Why not end it right now?

''Mother, we need to have a serious talk.''

''Yes, Aunt Lucy. About your funeral.'' Josh had always loved a good joke, but this was going too far. Matt shot him a murderous look.

''My *funeral?*''

''Yes, it's never too soon to plan.''

''But I'm not…''

''Not what, Mother?'' Matt stared her down, daring her to tell the truth.

''Not sure about the kind of funeral I want.''

''I'm the resident expert, I'll help you.'' Josh pulled up a chair. ''I was thinking something simple, no frills, no music.''

''No *music?*'' Lucy almost jumped out of bed, then caught herself.

Matt suppressed a smile. Count on Josh to provide comic relief.

''You want music?'' Josh said. ''How about something simple like 'Come Ye, Sinners'?''

''I was thinking about 'Seventy-six Trombones.'''

'''Seventy-six Trombones'?'' Matt all but yelled. His mother was serious.

"Yes. I'd like to think my passing will be occasion for a parade. You know…" She started singing in a lusty, off-key voice about seventy-six trombones leading a big parade. Then she caught herself and had a fake coughing spell.

"Here, Mother, let me help you." Matt patted her on the back with just enough force to make her think twice about pulling that stunt again.

"Thank you, dear. I'm quite all right now."

"You're sure?"

"Positive. About my funeral… Matt, you know I like ostentation. Josh, you ought to know it, too."

"Aunt Lucy, I'm just trying to help you go out with dignity. Look—" he held up a dress that even Matt with his nonexistent fashion sense could see was the ugliest garment he'd ever laid eyes on "—I rummaged around in your closet while you and Matt were discussing music and found this. It's perfect for you."

"I wouldn't wear that to the dogcatcher's."

"It's understated," Josh said.

"It's tacky. Your grandmother O'Banyon gave it to me one Christmas hoping I'd turn into some kind of uptight matron."

"You certainly didn't do that, did you, Mother?"

"For which we are eternally grateful," Josh said. "Now, Aunt Lucy, we need to discuss makeup."

"I want red lipstick. I look awful in pink."

"For the sake of dignity and economy, I was thinking we'd forgo makeup."

"No makeup? I look dead without makeup."

"Well, maybe a little powder."

"A little *powder?* Lord, I might as well be an elephant and go off into an elephant graveyard somewhere and just die."

"Now, Mother. Don't be so dramatic."

"Go away." Lucy put one arm over her eyes and waved them off. "I don't want to talk about this right now."

"We have to talk about it," Matt said. "After all, didn't you call me home to put all your affairs in order?"

He hoped Lucy would give up. He hoped she would tell the truth, admit her mistake, and then they could all stop the game of pretense.

"Well, yes, of course I did."

"All right then, I think I need to go ahead and make arrangements with the undertaker, look at some nice reasonably priced, no-frills caskets."

"No frills!" Lucy shut her eyes. "I'm going to take a little nap now. Please close the door on your way out."

"Let's see about that tea," Josh said, and Matt followed him to the kitchen, both of them holding in laughter until they got there.

Sandi whirled on them, still in high dudgeon. "I don't think it's very funny. If you ask me, all of us need to sit down and clear the air."

"Mother has to admit the truth."

"Do you?" Sandi glared at him.

"Do I what?"

"Always admit the truth?"

Matt felt gut-punched. With a look that would sear

a good brisket roast, Sandi marched out with her head held high.

"I see Aunt Lucy's plan worked."

"What do you mean?"

"There's more going on between you and the beautiful Sandi than a bit of playacting."

Matt didn't bother to reply. Over the last few days he'd been lied to, vamped, talked into trickery and deceit. He'd turned into a man who couldn't sleep, couldn't eat, couldn't think straight. He couldn't even control his own treacherous body.

"Did you come on your motorcycle?" he asked, and Josh lifted an eyebrow but didn't mention the abrupt subject change.

"I quit riding."

"Quit? Why?"

"My Harley's symbolic of my wild and woolly past. I'm trying to put all that behind me." He clapped his older cousin on the back. "Maybe you can give me a few pointers."

"I never sowed any wild oats."

"Never?"

Matt had a sudden vision of Sandi with her hair spread across the pillow and her legs wrapped around his waist.

"Let's drink our tea," he said. "Maybe it will wash the taste of dishonesty out of our mouths."

Sandi knocked on the connecting door, and Matt said, "Yes?"

"May I come in? I need to talk."

"Come in."

She pushed open the door and there he was, standing in front of the bed, shoeless, one sock off, one on. In spite of her robe and her noble intentions, she felt naked and fraudulent. Exposed.

His eyes raked over her and all of a sudden she wished she'd thought the whole thing through. She could have talked to him in the garden in broad daylight or even in the library after supper. Anywhere but here. Anyplace except this bedroom where he'd made her feel like a woman on a carousel circling the stars.

On the other hand, he'd avoided her all day. The last time she'd seen him was in the kitchen after their scene with Lucy, and she'd been in no mood to talk.

"If this is a bad time, I can come back later."

"No, this is fine. What did you want to talk about?"

"Lucy. I don't like doing what we did this morning."

"I don't like it either and I never should have involved you. I'm sorry, Sandi. Sorry for everything."

"Oh, I'm not sorry...."

"But you just said you were."

"Of course, I'm sorry about Lucy, but not about *everything*."

They stood very still, watching each other, desire hanging between them as thick and rich as honey. She waded toward him, heart-deep, one hand outstretched.

"Matt..." She touched his cheek, loving the virile, sandpapery feel of late-night beard stubble.

"You can leave O'Banyon Manor."

"You want me to go?"

"If you want to."

"I don't want to." Hand still on his cheek, she stood her ground, trembling.

"What do you want, Sandi?"

Everything. She wanted a family of her own to love, with fat-cheeked babies and two golden retrievers and aunts and uncles and a wonderful old house that said *welcome.* But most of all she wanted a man who would love her and cherish her the rest of her life.

She stared up at him. When he bent toward her, she saw everything in slow motion—the light in his eyes, the curve of his lower lip, the tiny star-shaped scar on his left jaw.

The kiss was deep and long, tender at first, quickly escalating to a passion so intense Sandi thought her frosty-pink toenail polish was going to melt. The rest of her had. She was nothing except a pulsing mass of longing.

His hands slid under her robe and found her aroused nipples through the silk of her gown. She pressed against him, writhing, mindless, inflamed. Fabric whispered to the floor.

As Matt picked her up and carried her to the bed, Sandi realized that this had been inevitable from the moment she opened the connecting door. *Why* didn't matter. The past, the future...nothing mattered except Matt and the magic she felt being in his arms.

His lips and hands touched her everywhere, searing her skin and igniting her body. She heard herself begging him for relief, pleading for release. He reached into the bedside table for protection.

"Anything for you, my love," he whispered, but before she could ask about his choice of words she succumbed to spasms of pleasure that drove everything else from her mind.

With all her senses fully aroused, she opened to the silver blessing of moonlight and the exotic fragrance of jasmine wafting through the window. She absorbed the light from Matt's eyes and the power from his taut muscles, exulted in the thick crisp texture of his hair, the sculpted beauty of his strong jaw.

The erotic journey they took was leisurely and reason-stealing, bold and tender, breathtakingly inventive and yet as old as time. He touched her in a thousand ways, but the one that stunned her most was the way he touched her heart and soul.

I'm in love. I love this man, truly love him.

Her newfound knowledge brought tears to her eyes. She was in love with a man who didn't love her, would never love her. And yet knowing that, she still wouldn't change a thing she'd done. How could she be sorry about losing her virginity in a romance-novel way on a sunset sail? How could she regret seeking shelter from the storm and finding it in Matt's arms? How could she be sorry that she'd come to find a way out of the tangled mess they were in and had instead found her heart?

She closed her eyes against the tears, against the glorious spasm of sensation. She shut her mouth against the words of love that wanted to tumble out, against the truth that was stamped on her heart, newly minted and bright as a silver dollar.

If she had been another kind of woman, a strong woman like C.J., Sandi might have leaped out of Matt's bed and said, "Wait a minute. What about love?" But she was a woman with a desperate need. Without the promise of forever, she needed to stretch the moment into morning so that when she left she'd have a night of passion to remember the rest of her life.

Liberated, a woman with nothing left to lose, she arched high, and when he rolled off, drained and depleted, she slid under the covers and brought him back to life.

With his hands around her waist he rolled onto his back and lifted her to the top of the world where she could almost see forever.

"What are you?" he murmured. "Some kind of sorceress?"

No. A woman in love. Keeping her secret, she leaned over him and stilled his questions with a kiss.

Lucy didn't have any qualms about knocking on doors waking up her friends.

Dolly came out of her bedroom complaining, "The last time I got rousted out of sleep at five o'clock in the morning it was for sex," and Kitty came out saying, "This had better be good."

Lucy took a detour by the kitchen for a bag of chips and three diet sodas, then they took the elevator down to the basement gym. Lucy ripped open the bag and mounted the treadmill with a double handful of chips.

"That's counterproductive," Kitty said.

"Who cares, when the whole world's falling down around my head?" Lucy consoled herself with chips.

"It's not the world, Lucy, it's your house of cards." Kitty dug into the chips while Dolly sipped her diet cola in silence.

"It feels like the whole world. I've lied to my only son and he's fixing to bury me in the ugliest dress I own."

"You're not dying," Kitty said.

"Thank God." Lucy climbed off the treadmill, winded. "Matt and Sandi act like they hate each other, Ben's coming soon and I need to be writing."

"The jig's up," Dolly said, deadpan.

"I couldn't have said it better myself," Lucy said.

"I can," Kitty said. "It's time for the truth, and not just about our silly matchmaking scheme."

Dolly banged her can down and headed for the door with Lucy calling after her, "Dolly? What's wrong?"

When Dolly turned around she looked fragile. "You don't need me for this discussion. The truth and I are strangers."

Lucy started after her, but Kitty put a hand on her arm. "Don't. She got news from her agent today."

"Bad news?"

"It all depends on your point of view. After she finishes filming her next picture, she'll be doing a stage play."

"That's great. Dolly loves the stage."

"In Washington, D.C."

Taking a handful of chips, Lucy passed the bag to Kitty. "We need these."

The two of them sat cross-legged on the floor, passing the bag back and forth until it was empty.

Vivid, erotic dreams and his own urgent need roused Matt from a deep sleep. "Sandi?" He reached across the bed and found it empty.

Naked and throbbing, he crashed back against the pillows and closed his eyes. What kind of fool was he? Not only had he wallowed all night long with a woman he'd had no business touching in the first place, but he'd been about to do the same thing all over again.

Groaning, Matt went into the bathroom and climbed into a shower so cold he got goose bumps. Shivering and scrubbing, he played mind games with himself.

Why would she leave his bed?

Fool. Why wouldn't she?

Was he that bad?

Arrogant fool.

After all he'd done, who could blame Sandi Wentworth if she sued him.

Even thinking her name opened a floodgate of emotions so unfamiliar to Matt that he cut himself shaving. He stanched the flow of blood with toilet paper, then dressed quickly and strode toward the connecting door.

His hand was already lifted to knock when he remembered the toilet paper. By the time he'd removed that badge of stupidity, he'd thought twice about what he was fixing to do.

If he barged into her room and found her, there

would be no way on heaven or earth he could prevent a repeat of last night's sorry performance. Not sorry in terms of sex, but sorry in terms of his motives.

What they'd done to and with and for each other had been phenomenal, magical, deserving of an award. But his reasons had been purely selfish and carnal.

Now he understood the phrase "the devil made me do it". It was man's way of refusing to take responsibility for his own actions.

Matt Coltrane was fixing to take responsibility. Right now. First he would find Sandi and apologize, then he would find his mother and tell her the game was over.

Sandi was driving and talking on her cell phone while C.J. kept saying, "Sandi? Honey, where are you? I can hardly hear you."

"I'm..." In a panic, Sandi realized she didn't even know where she was. "On the road."

"Where?"

"I don't know."

"Pull over. Sandi, honey, can you hear me? Pull over and stop somewhere until you quit crying. It's dangerous to drive in your condition."

Her condition. Sandi pulled off at a mom-and-pop store with a sign that said Eat. What was her condition?

"Sandi, did you pull over?"

"Yes."

"Okay. Take some deep breaths. Good. Now tell me what's wrong."

"I can't. I don't know. C.J., I need a place to stay for a few days and I don't want to go to my empty house."

"Come on. I'll get a supply of chocolate and popcorn."

"Clint won't mind?"

"Of course not. He's the most wonderful man in the world."

No, he's not. She'd just left the most wonderful man in the world asleep at O'Banyon Manor.

But Sandi didn't say so. Instead, she told C.J., "I'm on my way."

Chapter Nine

"You look awful," Lucy said.

She lowered her sunglasses and studied her son over the top. The last thing he'd expected was to find his mother by the pool in a bikini.

"Good God, Mother."

"Would you hand me the oil, dear? I think my belly's beginning to burn."

"What are you doing?"

"Sunbathing. What does it look like?" He handed her the oil then slumped into a lounge chair. "I figured this was as good a way as any to tell you I'm not dying."

"I know."

"You know?" He nodded. "When you and Josh were planning that dreadful funeral, you already knew, didn't you?"

"Yes."

"I don't know whether to laugh or cry."

Matt stared out over the pool while Lucy rubbed oil on her legs.

"I guess you know the rest of it, too?" she finally said.

"About how you tried to set me up with Sandi?"

"Oh, dear...what a terrible thing I've done to that lovely young woman."

You're not the only one, Matt wanted to say. But he didn't. He couldn't bear to think about just how hurtful his actions toward Sandi had been. And he couldn't even absolve himself with an apology.

He'd looked all over the house and grounds. Instead of finding the woman he'd sought, he'd stumbled upon his mother.

"Where is she?"

"Gone," Lucy said.

"What do you mean, gone?"

"She came early this morning to tell me that she was leaving."

"Leaving? She went into Shady Grove for the day?" Hopeful. That's what he was. Foolishly hopeful.

"No, dear, I'm afraid not. She came by to tell me she'd completed her sketching and didn't have to be here to finish the portrait."

He'd scared her off. And no wonder. What he'd done last night was unforgivable. Heady, mind-boggling, remarkable and unforgivable.

"Did she say where she was going?"

"No."

Naturally she wouldn't. It would be easy enough to find out where she lived. Without asking his mother. He would drive over and...

What? He couldn't seem to keep his hands off her, no matter how hard he tried.

"She'll be bringing the finished portrait back, I suppose." He tried to sound offhand, like a man whose heart was not in his throat.

"We didn't get into that. I imagine she'll call when it's finished and we'll go from there."

We'll go from there.

His mother and Sandi would, but what about him? What about Matt Coltrane who had sworn never to lose his heart? Where would he go now that Sandi Wentworth was under his skin and in his blood?

"I suppose she'll finish in a few days." Still hopeful. His mother saw right through him.

"You *did* fall in love with her."

"I don't believe in love."

"Darling, sometime or other everybody believes in love."

Matt stood up. This was not a discussion he wanted to have. Not now. Not with his heart raw and his nerves jangled. What he needed was sleep. He would pack his bag and head back to Jackson where his law practice waited and his life made sense.

"I have to be going, Mother."

"Matt, wait. There's something I have to tell you."

He was not up to any more true confessions. "We've said all we need to say today."

"It's about Sandi."

"What about her?"

"She left a message for you. She said to tell you she was sorry."

"Anything else?"

"No, that was all."

"You're sure?"

"Don't frown, dear. It makes you look old."

"Mother!"

"Yes, I'm positive. That's all she said." Lucy held out her hand. "Forgive me, Matt."

He bent down and kissed her cheek. "It's okay, Mother. I needed a break anyway."

"You're sure?"

"Positive. No harm done."

He hoped he was telling the truth. He hoped he had not done irreparable damage to the heart, mind or soul of the loveliest woman he'd ever met. The kindest, most generous woman he ever hoped to meet. The woman whose parting message was *I'm sorry.*

Sorry for what? Leaving? Staying too long? Sleeping with him? Not staying in his bed?

He had to find out.

On the long drive to Starkville, Sandi made up her mind that she wouldn't spoil her visit with her best friend by whining and crying. How many times had she running crying to C.J. with dashed hopes and romance gone awry?

"Too many," she said, talking to herself. It was

time to grow up, shape up, face her problems like a grown woman.

Sandi pulled over at a gas station, filled up, washed her face and bought a chocolate bar for comfort. On the road again, she did some serious thinking. The bottom line was that once again she had reached out like a starved child to a man who didn't want her. She had to quit that. She had to love her life, love herself and let some worthy man reach out to *her*.

But who? Who would seek out a woman her own mother couldn't love?

Certainly not Matt Coltrane. And he was the only man who counted, the only one she wanted.

Funny how you can go for years believing you know all about love, and then the real thing comes along and knocks you off your feet.

Well, she wasn't about to just lie there with her heart aching and her ego bruised. She was going to get up, brush herself off and get on with her life. She was going to quit attaching herself to other people's families and start a family of her own.

But not with a man. She was through with that, too. She was through searching for a man with father potential, when the world was filled with homeless babies just waiting for someone to love.

She would adopt. Single mothers did it all the time. She would go to China if necessary. Though she wasn't wealthy by any stretch of the imagination, she had the rest of her inheritance from her father. Somehow it seemed appropriate that the only family member who had ever loved her should be the means of giving her a family of her own.

She couldn't wait to tell C.J. the good news.

Sandi was not home. Either that, or she'd seen his car and wasn't coming to the door. Still, Matt stood on the empty front porch for five minutes knocking and calling her name. He hadn't earned the nickname Bulldog Coltrane for nothing.

He even went around to the back, never mind that somebody might mistake him for a burglar and call the police. The house was locked tight, no light showing underneath the windowsills, no sounds drifting out into the early evening.

Through the hedge he saw the little yellow cottage next door ablaze with lights. Neighbors that close would surely know her. They might even know where she was.

Matt took a shortcut through the hedge and was about to knock on the door, when he saw a sight that gave him pause—a woman dancing near-naked with a man wearing nothing but a top hat. As they twirled, the red scarves she held flew every which way and laughter drifted onto the front porch.

As Matt was backing off the front porch, he realized it was the couple who had been married by his mother's swimming pool. Sam Maxey and Ellie Jones.

Wouldn't you know?

But wait…wasn't it Sam's first wife, Phoebe, who had been like a mother to Sandi? It was his mother who'd told him. He'd been furious with her at the time, certain he already knew everything he needed to know about Sandi Wentworth, but now he vowed he would send his mother roses.

Sneaking like a thief in the night, he left the front porch, went back through the hedge, climbed into his car, then drove next door. He parked under Sam Maxey's magnolia tree and made a big to-do of slamming the car door and banging up the front-porch steps. All in slow motion.

Sam came to the door with his shirt buttoned wrong and no shoes. Ellie stood behind him in a robe with red scarves dripping out of the pockets.

"Why, it's Matt Coltrane." Ellie turned to her husband. "Darling, you remember Lucy's son?"

"Yes." Sam opened the door wide. "Won't you come in?"

"I'm sorry to barge in like this without calling, but I was looking for Sandi Wentworth."

"Oh, yes, Sandi," Sam said, beaming. "A lovely girl."

"Do you know where she is?"

Sam rubbed his chin. "We thought she was over at O'Banyon Manor."

Matt felt like a fool, an all-too-familiar state for him lately. If he didn't resolve this problem with Sandi soon, he might as well pull in his shingle and take up a job that required a lot of sweat and no brain.

"She left this morning," he said, "and she's not at home."

He was beginning to lose hope for his mission, then Ellie said, "She's probably at C.J.'s."

After he got the address, Matt struck out for Stark-ville like a teenager, without regard to time or planning. He was a man on a mission.

"Sweetheart, are you expecting anyone?" C.J. called toward the kitchen, and when her husband said, "No," Sandi got off the sofa as if she'd been pulled by strings and went to the front window.

Matt Coltrane was parked outside the small apartment, as big as life and twice as enticing. Her heart flew to her throat and her hand pressed there, hoping to keep it trapped inside.

C.J. came up behind her. "Sandi, what's the matter?"

"Do you want to see him?"

"No. Yes. I don't know."

"Make up your mind, quick. He's coming up the sidewalk. I'll get rid of him if you want me to."

"No, let him in. I've never run from anybody and I don't intend to start now." She smoothed her wrinkled shorts, wishing she'd changed out of her traveling clothes. She hadn't even combed her hair. It was flying every which way and she wasn't wearing a bit of lipstick. Not that it mattered. Why should it?

Matt Coltrane was nothing to her except the man she'd loved before she decided to quit giving her heart to men who didn't love her back. After a while a girl learns from unrequited love, if she'll let herself.

"All right then," C.J. said. "I'll let him in. You don't have to be in this room when he comes if you don't want to."

"Well, I'll just…" Sandi's mind turned in circles.

"Go." C.J. gave her a little push toward the bathroom. "I'll let him in, then Clint and I will vanish."

"You don't have to."

Just then, Clint stuck his head around the kitchen door. "I want to take my wife for walk in the moonlight so we can smooch."

The bell pinged through the apartment, making Sandi jump.

"Scoot." C.J. gave her the sign for victory, then opened the door to the one man in the world Sandi didn't want to see, the one man in the world she most wanted to see.

She leaned against the bathroom door, her eyes closed and her heart racing. What would she do when she saw him? What would she say?

Images of last night obscured everything else, and all she could think of was how he'd looked in the moonlight bending over her, smiling.

She heard his voice and it was like new wine in her veins, rich and heady. Drunk on the sound, she clamped her mouth against the moan that would give her away.

"I hate to barge in like this…"

Oh, she didn't hate it. She loved it. Loved that he'd cared enough to find out where she was, to follow her, to pound on the door of people who were virtual strangers to him. Could it mean that he cared? Did it mean that Matt Coltrane wasn't as immune to love as he professed?

Sandi forgot combs and lipstick and anything else

that would keep her apart from this wonderful man any longer. She left her hiding place wearing wrinkled shorts and a smile.

"Matt, what brings you here?"

"Sandi…" That smile. That beautiful smile. She read a thousand things into it and every one of them wonderful. "I came to see you."

"Won't you sit down?"

She sat on the sofa and he sat on a blue chair across the room. Where was C.J.? Why wasn't she taking up space in the blue chair, forcing Matt to sit beside Sandi on the sofa?

She glanced around for her vanished friend, suddenly wishing she'd asked her to stay, suddenly wanting an ally, a buffer, anyone, anything to stand between her and the man whose face had changed from soft to forbidding.

"You left without saying goodbye."

She imagined him in a courtroom intimidating opponents with that same stern look. Well, she wasn't about to be intimidated.

"Yes. It was time to go."

"Because of me?"

"Yes."

Well, there, she'd said it. The truth. She was too old for word games. Hated them, as a matter of fact. She was in this mess because of a silly game. Wouldn't the world be a better place if everybody just stopped pretending and said what they meant?

In a nice way, of course. In Sandi's book, there was no need to be unkind. Ever.

"I'm sorry," he said. "I didn't mean to hurt you, and I certainly didn't mean to scare you off."

"I didn't leave because I'm scared of you."

"Why, then?"

"I'm scared of me, of my own feelings."

Ask what they are. She sent him the silent message over and over, but he didn't hear. Or maybe he heard and chose to ignore it.

Sandi didn't press the issue. She would never speak of love until she believed there was at least a ghost of a chance that he was ready to hear.

"I see," he said, but of course, he didn't. She could tell by the puzzled look on his face.

They studied each other until the silence between them became unbearable.

"Can I get you something to drink?" she said. "Tea? Lemonade?"

"No, thank you. I have to be going."

"Oh…"

She knew how she sounded…like a little girl who has lost her favorite doll. She wished she were a better actress. She wished she could usher him out with the grace and style of a woman who, if she's not secure in the bosom of a loving family, is at least secure in her own company.

"Before I go…"

"Yes?"

Hope is a glorious thing, like a bird out of mating season who sings for no reason at all.

"Sandi, I want you to know that if there are any unforeseen developments from our being together—"

"Unforeseen *developments!*"

"Yes. If you should become pregnant, I will assume full financial responsibility."

Too enraged to speak, she glared at him as if he'd grown two heads. He had the grace to look uncomfortable.

"I should have thought of this earlier," he said.

"Thank God you didn't."

"Thank God I didn't?"

"Yes. If you'd made this *generous* offer at O'Banyon Manor I'd have…screamed."

"But, Sandi, be rational."

"You make me so mad. If I weren't such a lady I'd say an awful word. I'd *slap* you."

A big man riled is an awesome sight. Matt came out of his chair more tornado than man.

"You are the most unreasonable woman I've ever met. Look, Sandi, I know I must have sounded cold, but I'm only trying to be practical."

"You go on and be practical all by yourself, Matt. Forget about me, forget you ever saw me."

"That will be impossible to do." His gaze made her hot all over.

Oh, she wanted to believe that was true. She wanted to believe that he would lie sleepless in his bed, filled with the same love and wanting as she. She wanted to believe that memories would ambush him every day, that he would go to the kitchen for water then forget why he'd gone, that he would lose his train of thought in the midst of dictating important documents…even in the midst of ordinary conversation.

She was being a silly dreamer. It was time to face reality and get on with her life.

She took one last look at the man she loved, studied him with an artist's eye, imprinted every feature on her mind, seared every detail into her soul. Then she stood up and walked to the door.

"I'm sorry you made this long trip for nothing, Matt."

"Sandi…"

She waited, breathless. *It's not too late, Matt. One word of hope and I'm your slave forever.*

For a moment she thought he was going to say something important and wonderful, life-changing. Then he'd kiss her…

"Here's my number in case you ever need me." He handed her his business card.

"I won't need you, Matt."

He looked as if he was going to argue, but when she lifted her chin up, proud and stubborn, he walked past her and out the door. She closed it quickly. She couldn't bear to see him drive away, couldn't endure thinking that she'd never see Matt Coltrane again.

A hurting sound ripped through her and she slumped against the door, hand over her mouth. She stayed that way until the awful sounds stopped, until there was nothing in the small apartment except silence and leftover pain.

"I need you, Matt," she whispered. "I'll always need you."

Chapter Ten

"That didn't go well," Matt said as if he had an audience, somebody interested in his comings and goings, somebody who cared that five minutes ago he'd made a complete ass of himself in Starkville, Mississippi.

But only two people knew: the wonderful woman who by now was trying to forget she'd ever heard of him and Matt himself who was driving blindly toward Shady Grove as if his life depended on getting there within the hour, saying goodbye to his family then heading home to Jackson.

And probably it did. He needed routine. He needed safety. As mind-deadening and boring as it sounded to most folks, Matt thrived on a life without surprise. At the moment he didn't care if he never had another unexpected experience as long as he lived.

In fact, if he didn't know there would be backlogged cases stacked a mile high waiting on his desk, he'd probably hole up for a few days till he could learn to breathe again. Ever since Sandi Wentworth breezed into his life, he'd found himself sighing and groaning and laboring over what used to be a natural occurrence.

Even more important, he had to regain control. Thinking of how he'd lost it with Sandi, not merely once but repeatedly, Matt groaned. The unforeseen development he'd tried to discuss with her was a very real possibility. He'd never done anything that irresponsible. What had he been thinking?

Obviously, he hadn't. He was no longer capable of rational thought.

He had to get hold of himself. Preferably before he reached Shady Grove. Matt pulled over at the first motel he saw and checked in. Maybe tomorrow he'd be better able to face his family.

"How did it go?" C.J. asked. Clint had kissed them good-night, then slipped into bed so they could have some time alone. They sat cross-legged on the sofa sharing a big bowl of popcorn.

"Awful. I'm never going to see him again."

"But you want to."

"How can you tell?"

"I just can, that's all."

Of course she could. That's what friends did. Read minds and offered shoulders to cry on.

Sandi sighed. "He offered to pay me off in case I'm pregnant."

"Is that a possibility?"

For a moment Sandi got lost in delicious memories, and when she said yes, there were stars of hope in her eyes.

"Oh, C.J. Wouldn't it be wonderful?"

"It would be complicated, considering."

"You're right. I've got to quit fantasizing." She reached for a handful of popcorn, then munched awhile. "And I'm trying, really I am."

C.J. squeezed her hand. "You're doing fine, Sandi. We're here for you, and Sam and Ellie live right next door to you."

"I'm thinking of selling that house."

"Selling?"

"Yes, it's never been mine, not really. Grandmother's stamp is so strong I never felt I had the right to change anything."

"Well, good for you. I'm glad you're going to get rid of it. You can start fresh somewhere else. You can move down here and take an apartment close to Clint and me. That way you'll be here to help us build our dream house."

"Maybe I will. I don't know. First thing, though, is to go home and put the house on the market. Then I have to finish Lucy's portrait, and after that I'm going to China."

"You have an art show in China?"

"No, I'm going there to adopt a baby."

* * *

When Matt arrived midmorning there were so many vehicles parked around O'Banyon Manor, he became alarmed till he saw some of the logos. Van's Florist, Whitfield Caterers, Entertainment, Inc.

Lucy met him at the door. "Darling, you're back just in time."

"Mother, what's going on?"

"I'm getting ready for a party."

"What kind of party?"

"Who needs a reason to have a party, Matt? Call it anything you like. The I'm-not-dying party, the Ben-is-home party."

"Ben's back?"

"Yes." Lucy's cheeks were as pink as a girl's.

Matt studied his mother with newly aware eyes, but didn't say anything because quite frankly he didn't know what to say. He was the last person in the world to comment about matters of the heart, and from the looks of things, Lucy was involved in a matter of the heart.

"Where's Ben?" is all he said, and she flushed again.

"In the garden talking to the caterer."

Ben separated himself from the caterer when he saw Matt coming.

"Matt…" He extended his hand. "I owe you an apology and an explanation."

"An explanation will do."

"Lucy really did think she'd had a heart attack, and she was too embarrassed to admit her mistake."

"That sounds exactly like Mother."

"You know the rest of the story."

"Yes, except your part in it."

It was hard for Matt to reconcile Ben's complicity in his mother's foolish plan with the dependable, honest, steady man.

"Yes, I can see how that would puzzle you." Ben pulled off his glasses and polished them with a pristine handkerchief he pulled out of his pants pocket. "I can never refuse anything Lucy asks of me." He put his glasses back on and looked Matt squarely in the eye. "I've been in love with your mother for years. Long before Henry Coltrane came along and fed her a line of bull."

Matt appraised the older man in the unforgiving light of a bright summer's day. He had a full head of hair, dark brown with gray streaks that looked silver in the sun. Dark, intelligent eyes that missed nothing. A wide and ready smile. Body tanned and fit.

Altogether he was quite an impressive figure. He could see how Ben might turn a woman's head. But there was something else Matt knew about this old family friend: he was kind, compassionate and loyal, not at all the kind of man who would use his office as a playground for half the women in Shady Grove.

Matt could see how Lucy could love Ben and why it might work.

"You have my blessing," he said.

"Thank you, Matt, but that's a bit premature. Until Lucy admits what happened with Henry, there's no room for me in her life."

"Aunt Kitty knows. Probably Aunt Dolly and the rest of the Foxes."

"I'm talking about you, Matt. You don't know how many times I've wanted to come to you and say, 'Look, son, you don't have to carry this burden.' She's the only one who can do that. She's the only one who can relieve you of it."

"It's over and done with. Might as well let sleeping dogs lie, isn't that what they say?"

"They do." He patted Matt's shoulder. "But I never subscribed to collective wisdom." Spotting Lucy in the garden, Ben smiled. "There she is. Have you ever seen a more wonderful woman?"

Matt had a sudden vision of Sandi, which he quickly shoved out of his mind.

"No," he said. "I don't think so."

If Matt were female, folks would call him a wallflower, but that was fine with him. He preferred standing in a quiet corner watching the party from afar.

Josh came through the French doors, backlit by Japanese lanterns the decorators had hung over the courtyard and a moon as big as Texas.

"I thought I'd find you in here." He handed Matt a glass of wine, then straddled a chair facing him. "Do you want to talk about Sandi?"

"No."

"Believe it or not, I've become pretty good at dispensing advice."

"You were always good at that."

"Yeah, but it wasn't always wise."

Matt began to feel uncomfortable with his cousin, an entirely new sensation for him. He'd always been at ease no matter where he was, and especially with the lovable, easygoing Josh. Still, there was something about his cousin's intense scrutiny that made Matt feel exposed and vulnerable.

"Aunt Kitty says you're leaving tomorrow," Matt said.

"Yep. How about you?"

"Same. I talked to my secretary today. The partners are going crazy taking up my slack." He walked to the door and watched his mother dancing with Ben. In the moonlight, laughing, she looked like a young girl.

They'll be good for each other, he thought, and then he didn't let himself think about anything else. Not his father, not the past, not Sandi, not anything.

He turned back to Josh and said, "How about a game of billiards?"

Josh grinned. "It's as good a way as any to make our escape," he said.

In the basement with nothing but the sound of the pool cue snapping the balls and Josh's deep voice turning parish stories into high comedy, Matt passed the time until he could make his final escape.

Back to the sanity of his law practice in Jackson.

Matt turned the page of his daily planner with some satisfaction. Another day gone by. And he'd only thought about Sandi Wentworth five times—when he'd woken up in his bed alone, when he'd passed a car that looked like hers on the way to work, when he'd had the bad luck to get a waitress at lunch with blond hair, when he'd made the mistake of glancing out his window at the sunset, and worst of all, when he'd been in the middle of talking to his partner Bob about the case against the hospital.

That had been embarrassing. No, humiliating. He'd been talking about the tort case and then he'd been struck dumb by a memory of Sandi on the sailboat.

"Matt?" Bob had said. "Are you all right?"

"Yes. Just a touch of indigestion."

"Yeah, I know. Chinese food will do that to you. All that MSG."

Thank God Bob was a health-food nut. He'd launched into a windy lecture about food additives that had lasted until Matt could get himself together.

He placed his daily planner in the center of his desk where he'd see it first thing tomorrow, then picked up his briefcase and headed home. He'd warm a TV dinner in the microwave. No sense risking another waitress with golden hair. No sense driving through streets where three dozen cars like hers could sneak up on him and drive him crazy.

He ate his dinner that tasted like cardboard, watched a game show he hated and a movie he didn't even know the title of, then brushed his teeth and climbed into his tidy bed. Nobody on the other side to hog the covers, no alluring perfume to steal his sleep, no soft body curved close to steal his senses.

"Two weeks down and a lifetime to go," he said, then he stared at the clock while the neon hands mocked him.

Being caught up in a whirlwind didn't give a girl time to think about her problems, which was fine with Sandi. In the eight weeks since she'd left O'Banyon Manor she had nearly finished Lucy's portrait, put her house on the market, moved into the apartment next to C.J. and Clint and set the adoption of a Chinese girl into motion.

C.J. and Clint had a celebration party for her, and when Sandi asked, "For which big event?" C.J. said, "Take your pick."

"Motherhood."

"I thought so."

Some of C.J.'s classmates in the vet school came, one of them a very interesting, studious-looking guy from Kentucky who kept trying to get Sandi off by herself.

"Buck's a really nice guy," C.J. told her when they caught a private moment in the kitchen. "And he loves children."

"I know. I told him about my little girl, and he seemed genuinely thrilled for me."

"Well?"

"He has a great smile, he's thoughtful and he's a good conversationalist."

"But?"

"How did you know there was a *but?*"

"Because I know you, Sandi."

"Okay, as foolish as it is, he's not Matt."

"I thought so."

C.J. put her glass on the table and caught Sandi's hands. "Listen to me, sweetie. It's okay to love a man who's hard to catch. Lord knows, I thought Clint Garrett would never see the light."

"But he did."

"Yes, he did."

"But Clint's more…oh, I don't know…laid-back than Matt. He has this great legal mind and he keeps trying to organize every event in his life into neat little files."

"I'll bet you blew his mind!"

Clint joined them in the kitchen. "You two are having more fun in here than all the rest of them put together." He slid his arms around C.J. and nabbed a chocolate-dipped strawberry, which he promptly fed to his wife.

Jealousy stabbed Sandi, just a tiny bit, but still she was ashamed of herself. She was happy for C.J., she really was. And yet seeing her with an adoring husband set up an ache in Sandi that was almost physical.

All the empty spaces that Matt had once filled were suddenly screaming for attention. And maybe Buck could provide that.

But if Sandi went flying off in his direction simply because he was an available nice guy, then she was moving backward instead of forward. She was letting herself get caught up in old patterns that had always been her undoing.

Clint's strawberry quickly led to kisses that needed

some privacy, so Sandi told the lovebirds, "I'm going back to the party."

They broke apart long enough for C.J. to say, "Have fun."

"I will," Sandi said. But not with Buck. No, when she joined the party, she spotted him beside C.J.'s potted palm looking hopeful, and she deliberately went in the other direction.

Matt's secretary buzzed him in the middle of one of the most hectic days he could remember in about five years.

"It's your mother."

Lucy didn't call at the office unless she had some sort of emergency. He grabbed the phone.

"Mother, what's wrong?"

"Nothing, dear, I just wanted to invite you up for the weekend."

"Why didn't you tell me when I called this morning?"

Since his return from taking care of his *dying* mother's business, Matt had tried to pay more attention to Lucy. He called her every morning right after his coffee, and he made a point to visit at least once a month.

He'd been in Shady Grove a week ago and hadn't planned on going back for at least two.

"I didn't tell you because I didn't know this morning," Lucy said, as if that made a lick of sense to Matt.

"You didn't know what?"

"About Sandi coming. She's finished my portrait

and I invited her to stay for the whole weekend. She said yes.''

Matt's heart did a funny trip-hammer flip-flop, but he wasn't about to pay attention to anything as fickle and frivolous as the heart.

"That's nice," he said. "You two will enjoy each other's company."

"You're not coming?"

"No, Mother. I'm not coming."

"But I thought you'd want to. I mean…after all the fun we had the last time."

"Fun!"

"I know it got a little out of hand, but still, you'd have to say that we had a lively time together and, believe it or not, those times are hard to come by. Not just everybody has the capacity for joy, but of course, Sandi, being an artist—"

"Mother, save your breath. I'm not coming."

"Is that final?"

"It's final."

Lucy sighed. "Well, is there anything you want me to tell her?"

"Tell her…" What? How she'd ruined his ability to get a good night's sleep? How she'd destroyed his concentration? "Nothing," he said. "Don't tell her anything."

After their last time together, she probably wouldn't even want to hear the mention of his name.

"Is Matt here?"

Those were the first words out of Sandi's mouth,

and fortunately she'd said them to the fun-loving, compassionate Lucy instead of the gardener or the maid or some perfect stranger who happened to answer the door.

As far-fetched as that sounded, it was certainly a possibility. Dolly and a cast and crew from Hollywood were staying at O'Banyon Manor filming a scene for her latest movie. A minor detail Lucy had failed to mention when she'd issued the weekend invitation.

"No, dear, I'm afraid he won't be coming. He's very sorry he couldn't make it, though."

"He is?"

"Oh, I'm sure of it."

Sandi floated upstairs on that bit of good news, following Lucy to a room that was heart-stoppingly familiar.

"Every room in the house is occupied. I'm putting you here. I hope you don't mind."

"No, of course not."

Mind? She was ecstatic. After Lucy left she went around Matt's bedroom caressing furniture and mooning over selected portions of the Oriental carpet. *Here,* her gown on the floor with his pants. *Here,* his socks abandoned while they made love. *Here,* his pillow. *Here,* the sheets that had covered them while they kept the storm at bay.

Oh, she couldn't wait for bedtime. She couldn't wait to climb into that wonderful, history-laden four-poster bed. She was going to climb in buck naked, wallow around in the cool sheets and hot memories arousing

her and pretend that she was waiting for Matt to return
so she could give birth.

"No, no," she would tell the doctor. "I can't do
this till my husband gets here. He wants to see the
birth of his first baby right in the same bed where he
was born."

She didn't know that for sure, of course, but why
couldn't it be true? Naturally her husband would want
his son to be born there. Naturally he would want his
wife to follow the long line of O'Banyon women
who—

"Sandi? Dinnertime. Are you okay?" It was Dolly
outside in the hallway, knocking and calling her name.

Chagrined, Sandi opened the door. "I'm sorry. I'm
so excited to be back I got carried away and forgot
the time."

"That's the way I feel every single time I come
back. Like being welcomed home."

"Exactly."

Arm in arm, the two women went down to dinner.

If anybody had cared enough to ask why he was on
the road in the middle of the night headed to Shady
Grove, hell-bent for leather, Matt would have said,
"Insanity." That was the only explanation he could
think of for getting up in the middle of a fairly decent
movie he'd rented, leaving a half-eaten pizza on the
coffee table and packing his bag.

It wouldn't hurt to visit his mother more than once
a month is what he told himself. Lord knows he wasn't

much else except a good lawyer. He might as well try to be a dutiful son.

Of course, there were his sisters. He did all right by Elizabeth and Jolie when he saw them, which wasn't much.

"Face it, old boy," he said. "You're all alone."

Here he was talking to himself, though he wasn't going to mentally flagellate himself over that. The Natchez Trace Parkway did that to lots of people. Once an Indian trade route between Nashville, Tennessee, and Natchez, Mississippi, the Trace was now a controlled-access federal parkway with a speed limit designed for sightseers and the patrolmen who delighted in catching lawyers who ought to know better than to go sixty-five miles an hour instead of the lawful fifty.

The speeding ticket irked Matt. It was his first since he was a kid with a new driver's license and a yen for some reckless fun.

He didn't like to think about why he'd been speeding, any more than he wanted to contemplate his hasty decision to visit his mother. If he had a lick of sense left he'd have turned and gone back home when he was only twenty minutes on the road.

But no, he was now more than halfway to Shady Grove, so he planned to make the best of it. He'd slip quietly into his bed, make a few pleasant remarks to Sandi in the morning, then call home for messages and leave saying he had urgent business to attend to, sorry to cut the weekend short, that sort of thing.

It was a good plan. And he was going to stick to it. No matter what.

Feeling better now that he had a course of action, Matt turned on the radio and whistled along to the first two tunes, which he happened to know. He didn't know the next one nor the ten after that, and all of a sudden it struck him as sad that he didn't know the tunes to songs that half the people in Jackson hummed on their way to work. What did that say about a man?

That his life was damn narrow, for one thing. And that it was pretty empty if it didn't even have music.

Right then and there he made up his mind that when he got back to Jackson he was going to purchase a CD player with the best set of speakers on the market, then go into a good music store and get the latest of everything—blues, jazz, rock and roll, rap. You name it, Matt Coltrane was going to buy it.

And by George, the next time he found himself on the road all alone late at night, he was going to whistle along to every damn song on the radio.

''That'll show them,'' he snarled, though he had no idea who he'd be showing nor why he nearly tore the knob off when he shut off the radio.

His dark mood didn't lessen all the way to Shady Grove, and when he drove up in his mother's yard and saw about two dozen vans and cars and trucks, his attitude turned positively vile.

Wasn't that just like Lucy to plan a big party for Sandi? Peacocks from all over Shady Grove would be there strutting around, showing off their colors, trying to catch her eye.

Well, let them. He'd stand back and watch and not lift a finger even if she wanted him to.

He jerked his bag out of the car and banged his shin. Hard. It took considerable effort not to stand there in the dark cussing.

He wouldn't lower himself to that. He'd show them all. Matt Coltrane was a man in total control.

The house was dark, everybody sleeping, thank God. He wasn't up to an inquisition tonight.

He stood letting his eyes adjust to the dark before he headed toward the stairs. He didn't want to trip over any furniture left out of place by late-night revelers.

Why Lucy had invited them all to spend the night was beyond his comprehension. None of it made any sense. He wished he'd taken a closer look at the license plates, but he wasn't about to go poking around outside at this late hour. He probably couldn't see them anyway. It was one of those starless nights with a bottomless black sky.

All he wanted was to fall into his bed and try to sleep. Maybe being back at O'Banyon Manor would work like a sleeping narcotic to cure his recent insomnia. He could use about four straight weeks of sleep.

Since his mother's house was full of people, he sneaked into his own room, not even turning on the lights lest he wake a perfect stranger. He didn't even bother to put his bag in the closet, just stripped off his clothes and climbed into bed then fell gratefully toward his pillow.

That was more like it. A man could sleep in a bed like this. Settling in, getting comfortable, Matt rolled to his side…and into the soft arms of a sleeping woman.

"Hmm?"

The sleepy female voice lit firecrackers inside him, and he shot out of bed as if it were occupied by man-eating barracudas.

"What the hell?"

He snapped on the light and Sandi sat up wearing nothing except an expression of surprise.

"Matt? What are you doing here?"

"More to the point, what are *you* doing here?"

"Sleeping…until you came along."

"You don't have to act so huffy about it. This *is* my bedroom."

"It's the only one available."

"I see."

Actually he was seeing more than he wanted to. All that lovely flushed skin, the rosy nipples tightly puckered, the tiny nipped-in waist, the cute belly button that he wanted to lick.

God.

"Where are your clothes?"

"I'm not wearing any," she said.

She took her sweet time pulling up the sheet. Belatedly he realized he was standing there stark naked, watching. He pounced on his briefs, wishing fervently he was the kind of man who wore baggy boxers so he could hide at least some of his embarrassing condition.

He breathed deeply three times, then turned back around to find her wide-eyed and pink-cheeked, irresistible. Almost.

"It seems we're stuck with each other," he said, and when she blushed, he regretted his poor choice of words.

"Yes."

God. How many ways could this sleepy, disheveled woman seduce him?

"I'll sleep in the chair." He headed that way. All business.

"No, let me." She leaped out of bed, then hopped back in and wrapped the sheet all the way up to her neck. But not before he'd seen everything he'd ever wanted.

"Stay put."

"You don't have to roar," she said.

Matt counted to ten. "You're already settled in, so please just lie back down and go to sleep."

"But the chair is so small and you're so *big*."

She had this engaging way of slipping her pink tongue over her lower lip when she was unsure of herself. Pierced, he stalked across the room and snapped off the light in self-defense.

"Tonight won't be the first time I've slept in a chair."

"Well, then, if you're sure."

"I'm positive. Go to sleep, Sandi."

He felt around the top of the closet for a quilt, snapped it open then wadded himself into a space that would have been perfectly comfortable for a five-year-old. Dreams of a good night's sleep now in tatters, he gritted his teeth, shut his eyes and tried to make the best of it.

"Matt?"

He jerked up and pulled a crick in his neck. "What?"

"You don't have to yell."

"I'm not yelling. I'm asking you politely, what do you want?"

"I don't *want* anything. I was just saying good-night."

"Good night, Sandi."

He pulled the quilt around his ears, uncovering his feet in the process. Well, hell, let them stick out. There were worse things than cold feet.

Sleeping in the same room with Sandi Wentworth and not being able to touch her, for one thing. Good Lord, what was the matter with him? And why in the world hadn't he turned around and gone to a motel the minute he discovered her in his bed?

Insanity. The woman was driving him stark raving mad.

Unhinged, he lay there trying to decide whether to go or stay. If he left now, after making such a big to-do of sleeping on the chair, she'd think he was running away from her.

Well, he'd have her know that Matt Coltrane didn't flee from anybody, and that included enticing wenches with tangled golden hair, innocent-looking eyes and a body designed by somebody who obviously had a cruel sense of humor. Why else would the only woman on the planet he absolutely, positively could not resist be put in his path looking like that?

"Matt?"

He jerked up so fast he banged his knee on the marble-topped table beside the lounge chair. Matt counted slowly to ten before he answered her.

"What?" he said, just as sweet as pie.

"Are you all right over there?"

"Yes." What did she mean by that? "Why shouldn't I be?"

"Well, you keep tossing and turning."

"Sorry if I'm keeping you awake."

"Oh, no, it's not that. I just thought you might want to change places. I'm smaller, you know."

"I know."

He could measure her with his hands. And had. The precise length and breadth and depth of her was seared into his memory.

"Thanks for the offer," he said. "Just go to sleep, Sandi."

"Okay. 'Night, Matt."

"Good night *again*."

She lay perfectly still until she heard the even sound of his breathing. Oh, she felt dreadful taking his bed, and selfish to the core. Squinting till her eyes became adjusted to the dark, she saw how uncomfortable he looked, legs jackknifed off the chair, one arm crushed behind his head, the other hanging nearly to the floor.

And with only one quilt. The least she could do was make sure he didn't get cold.

Easing out of bed so she wouldn't wake him, Sandi slid her quilt off the bed and tiptoed across the room to cover him. He stirred but didn't wake up.

She made sure his feet were covered, then stood there telling herself she absolutely must not brush his hair back from his face. Oh, but she could look, couldn't she? She could drink her fill of the man who overflowed her heart so that she wondered she didn't leave a trail of love everywhere she went.

A small sigh escaped her, and he mumbled in his sleep. She still wasn't wearing a stitch. What if he woke up and caught her staring at him? What would he think? What would he do?

If she went rummaging around in the dark for her gown, she'd surely wake him, and they'd be right back where they started. Holding her breath, Sandi tiptoed to bed, eased under the sheet and lay there trying to fall back to sleep.

It was impossible, of course. She never could sleep when she was cold. Maybe she should check the closet and see if she could find another quilt. But no, then there would be the same problem of being caught awake, naked.

She would just have to make the best of the situation, that was all. There were worse things than freezing to death alone in Matt's bed while he slept nearby under two quilts. But she couldn't think what they were.

Whoever invented air-conditioning with lying thermostats that said seventy but felt like sixty ought to be shot. Sandi would write a letter if she knew where to send her complaint.

She tried wrapping her arms around herself, then she tried curling into a ball, then she pulled the sheet over her head. Nothing helped.

She was doomed to spend the rest of the night awake and shivering.

Pinpricks in his left leg woke Matt up. Somehow the leg was wedged under him and was now a dead weight with absolutely no feeling, as if it had been amputated.

Stretching and rubbing his leg, Matt noticed the extra quilt. No wonder he'd felt toasty. Too hot, as a matter of fact.

Sandi must have put the quilt there.

He squinted toward the bed till he could make her out, a small huddled form looking no bigger than a kitten in the middle of his large antique bed. She was probably freezing. Women were like that. Or so he'd been told.

The feeling was coming back. Matt tested his leg against the floor, found it secure and tiptoed over to the bed with the extra quilt. Bending over, he gently tucked it around her.

She heaved a little sigh, uncurled her legs and rolled to her side with one hand tucked under her cheek. She was smiling.

She was beautiful.

She was irresistible.

Being very careful, Matt lifted a strand of golden hair that had fallen across her cheek. It was silky and liquid-feeling, like something alive.

He stood there with his hand suspended over her face while the soft strand of hair drifted through his fingers.

It suddenly struck him as remarkable that a woman as kind and gentle as Sandi Wentworth was alone in the world. What had been wrong with her three fiancés? Hadn't they known they were holding pure gold in their hands?

If Matt had anything to offer her, he'd go after her in a heartbeat. But she deserved more than cynicism and coldness. She deserved more than a guilt-racked man who had lied to a worthy mother in order to protect an unworthy father.

Standing beside the bed watching her sleep, he lost track of time. She made a little moaning sound and he wondered, was she cold?

He tiptoed back across the room, retrieved the other quilt and tucked it tenderly around her. A streak of rosy gold from the rising sun fell across her cheek. Soon it would be dawn. No sense trying to go back to sleep.

It wouldn't work anyhow. Not with this aching vision of Sandi in his head.

He held vigil over her until dawn crept over the windowsill, then he sneaked back to his chair and feigned sleep so she wouldn't wake up and feel guilty.

He heard her the minute she woke up. Out of the corner of his eye he saw her sit up in bed and stretch, her skin deliciously flushed and her eyes bright with morning.

She tiptoed to her suitcase and pulled on a robe, and he could no longer pretend. He sat up rubbing his eyes as if he'd just had the best night's sleep of his life.

"Good morning," she said. "Did you sleep well?"

"Like a rock."

She didn't believe him. He'd read enough faces in a court of law to know.

"Do you mind if I shower first?" she said.

He pictured Sandi in the bathroom, wet and naked.

"Go ahead. I'm going down to the pool to do a few laps."

"That sounds like fun."

Was she angling for an invitation? That's all he needed.

"Not the way I swim," he said. "I do serious laps. It's a tough workout."

"Your body shows it."

Why was it the least little thing she said was a turn-on for him? He told her thanks a little too curtly, he was sorry to say. Then he turned his back on the enchantress and rammed his toned but aching body into a pair of jeans.

"Matt?"

He turned around shirtless then wished he hadn't. The way she was staring at his chest made him long for things he knew he couldn't have. He got caught up in her soft, wanting look, and for an instant he thought about taking her in his arms and leading her to the bed where they would make slow, sweet love to greet the morning. The very best kind.

Fortunately his common sense reasserted itself, and he dragged himself out of his desire-induced stupor to say, "What, Sandi?"

"Your mother invited me here for the entire weekend."

"I know."

She caught her delicious pink tongue between her lips in that unstudied pose that drove him mad. He covered his condition, now acute, by turning sideways and putting on a shirt.

"I'll take a hotel room tonight," she said.

"Absolutely not." *Breathe,* he told himself. "You're Mother's guest, and you will stay here. *I'll* take the hotel room."

"Oh, no. I couldn't possibly let you do that. Why, I'd feel awful, chasing you out of your own home!"

"No one chases me, Sandi. I make decisions and stick to them. I'll get a room in town tonight."

"Oh, I can't disappoint Lucy that way. I'll just tell her something came up and I have to leave."

"No. I insist you stay." Why didn't he let her go? Why couldn't he? "For Mother's sake."

"I'll stay if you will."

"That's emotional blackmail."

"I just want everybody to be happy, that's all."

"Sandi, you're a sweet woman. Probably too sweet for your own good."

The smile she gave him was full of wicked good humor. "Maybe I should transform myself. Maybe I'll dye my hair red and become a witchy kind of woman who drives men mad."

God, if she drove him any madder, he'd have to be put in a straitjacket.

"Don't change. Promise me."

"If you'll promise to stay."

"Deal," he said.

Why did he get the sinking feeling that the new deal he'd struck with her would be as disastrous as the first?

Chapter Eleven

Matt found his mother in the sunroom having a late breakfast.

"Matt. I'm so glad you decided to come." Lucy didn't have to stand on tiptoe to kiss her son because she was wearing the kind of shoes that caused unnecessary falls, big lawsuits and handsome settlements.

"Mother, you're going to fall and hurt yourself on those things. What are you doing wearing shoes like those?"

"I'm in a party mood. If you're going to be a sourpuss, just go back to Jackson." She patted his cheek to show she didn't mean what she'd said. "Sit down and eat, dear. You look dreadful. Is anything wrong?"

"What could possibly be wrong?"

He didn't miss the sly look in Lucy's eyes. "Did you sleep well?"

"Like a brick."

"Oh, good. Sandi, too?"

"You planned this, didn't you, Mother? And don't try to play innocent. You deliberately put her in my room."

"The house is filled, dear, and you said you weren't coming. Would you rather have walked in on Chris DeClair?"

"That depends. Who is she?"

"Not *she. He*. He's directing Dolly's picture. A terrific man. They're in the gazebo. Sandi's with them."

Matt pictured him, twenty-seven, slicked-back hair, charming, the kind of man who kissed women's hands and told them lies. Matt had tennis shoes older than some of those Hollywood directors.

"That should please Aunt Dolly, working for a young director."

He shoved back his plate and stood up.

"Where are you going, dear?"

"I haven't seen Dolly yet."

Chris was looking at Sandi the way she figured he might look at lobsters that restaurants kept in tanks so the customers could pick out the ones they considered most succulent. Besides that, he kept edging his chair closer so his legs touched hers.

She ought to be flattered. Instead, she felt uncomfortable. She tried to think of some remark that would be clever but discouraging, but she didn't want to hurt his feelings, especially since she was a guest in Lucy's house. And besides, she didn't know the first thing about putdowns, clever or otherwise.

"There's Matt," Dolly said, then left her chair to give him a hug.

Saved, Sandi thought, which was an odd way to view him considering their brief history. She was halfway out of her chair when she saw the scowl on his face.

Probably because of her. After all, she'd deprived him of his bed and probably his sleep.

She settled back into her chair, and then Chris leaned over and said, "Look, we're not filming today. How about the two of us sneaking off for a bite of lunch? I hear the barbecue in Mississippi is fantastic."

"I know just the place," she said.

When she stood up, Chris put his arm around her waist and she let him. Not that she meant to embark on another of her whirlwind romances, for goodness' sake. And certainly not that she wanted to make Matt Coltrane jealous.

She wasn't that kind of woman, and besides, the man could barely stand the sight of her. He wouldn't notice if she went to lunch with the whole army brass band.

Still, there was something dark and dangerous in his eyes now, something that made her shiver.

"You're leaving?" Matt's inquiry was polite and cold enough to freeze her eyelashes.

"We're going to the pool hall for barbecue."

"Enjoy."

"Oh, I plan to."

"Great. We want all the guests of O'Banyon Manor to have a good time."

"Thank you."

She couldn't look away from his eyes, couldn't move. Chris began to shift from one foot to the other, obviously uncomfortable with the fearsome-looking son of his hostess.

Matt stuck out his hand to Chris. Belatedly, Sandi thought.

"Matt Coltrane. If you need anything just let me know."

"I think I have everything I want, thanks."

The tension was so thick Sandi could taste it, like lightning in the air, close and ready to strike.

"Good. Take care." Matt wheeled around and strode toward the house.

"What was that all about?" Chris asked.

"Who knows? Let's eat."

Indeed, what was it all about?

After she'd made it clear she didn't want his hands on her, Chris turned out to be a good companion, fun, entertaining, easygoing. He suggested a movie after lunch, one she hadn't seen, and his commentary made it so interesting she didn't protest when he said, "Let's see some more."

In between features she called Lucy. "Don't wait dinner," she said.

"We don't mind, dear."

"No, please. Chris and I are going to be very late."

"I hope you're having fun."

"Yes, we're at the movies. He knows so *much*. I'm seeing them in a new way."

"Good. Sandi, hold on a minute, dear. What was that, Matt?"

Sandi couldn't make out what he was saying, but the sound of his deep voice was enough to turn her insides to butter and make her close her eyes, wishing. She wished they'd met under different circumstances. She wished they'd never been so caught up in the game they didn't see each other, *really* see each other. She wished Matt had fallen in love with her.

But oh, she didn't regret the time she'd had with him, not one minute of it. She hugged herself, holding the precious memories close.

She was making changes, turning her life inside out and upside down, but no matter what happened, no matter where she went or who she was with, she'd always remember Matt. She'd always hold him above the rest, special in ways it would take her days to tell, years, lifetimes.

"Sandi, are you still there?"

"I'm here, Lucy. Sorry."

"Are you all right, dear?" Lucy said, and hard on her heels came Matt's voice.

"What's wrong? If something's happened to Sandi…"

The rest was muffled. Probably Lucy had put her hand over the receiver.

What, Matt? What would you do?

Sandi closed her eyes, dreaming.

"Sandi?" It was Chris, tapping on the phone booth.

"Movie's about to start. We don't want to miss the beginning."

She cracked open the door. "Go ahead. I'll join you."

Chris nodded, gave her a thumb's-up, then headed back into the theater.

"Sandi?" Lucy was back. "Take your time, have fun, stay as long as you like. I'll leave the front door open."

"I don't want to cause you any trouble."

"It's no trouble. This is Shady Grove and besides I've always contended that if a burglar wants in, a lock is not going to stop him."

Sandi heard the deep rumble of Matt's voice once more, and even after Lucy said goodbye and hung up, she sat in the phone booth dreamy-eyed, wishing he would be the one waiting for her in the theater. She pictured how it would be: they'd sit in the dark holding hands, thighs touching, reveling in each other. Sexual tension would build and build, but they'd hold it in, satisfying themselves with a stolen kiss or two, mouths open, tongues engaged. She'd tingle all over and pretend to watch the show, but all the time her mind would be filled with Matt, only Matt.

Sighing, she left the phone booth and went to join Chris.

It would be foolish to wait up for her. That's what Matt told himself. It would send the wrong signal.

Equally foolish to sleep in the chair when he could grab an hour on the bed. He was a light sleeper, es-

pecially lately. He'd hear her coming in time to leap
into the chair, pull up the quilt and pretend to be sound
asleep.

What had he been thinking of, anyway, agreeing to
stay? He hadn't promised to stay in his bedroom, and
had actually planned to bunk on the sofa in the library,
but no, six of the film crew were down there engaged
in a game of poker that looked as if it would last all
night.

Besides, Matt didn't want to risk being caught in
the morning by some nosy guest who would wonder
why he was sleeping on the couch.

What was keeping Sandi so long, anyhow? Didn't
the theater close at one?

Dolly had assured him Chris was harmless as a
puppy, but puppies sometimes licked you all over,
didn't they? Climbed up in your lap and wanted to be
cuddled?

Matt paced his room till he was bleary-eyed from
lack of sleep and worry. At the rate he was going,
he'd fall asleep at the wheel tomorrow driving back to
Jackson.

He didn't know what woke him. The fragrance of
gardenia or the feel of soft flesh pressed against him.
Momentarily disoriented, he stared into the darkness
until he made out the bedposts. He was at O'Banyon
Manor.

And the woman in his arms was Sandi Wentworth.
He stared at the face only inches from his, long eyelashes resting against cheeks as pink as a damask rose,

silky hair fanned across the pillow, perfect lips slightly parted and dewy looking. As if they'd recently been kissed.

A fury unlike any he'd ever known built in Matt. He was *jealous*. He couldn't believe it. Jealousy was a petty, unworthy emotion and he wasn't about to fall victim to such messy feelings.

What he would do was ease out of bed, creep over to the chair, crawl under the quilt and stay there till morning. He glanced at the clock. It was only another two hours away. He could endure anything for two hours, even lying only three feet from Sandi without touching her.

God, she felt wonderful. And she was sleeping deeply. He caressed her arm with his fingertips, and it wasn't enough. It wasn't nearly enough.

Tenderly he brushed her hair back from her face then traced the soft curve of her cheek, the sweet line of her jaw, the irresistible pout on her lips.

He wanted to make love with her. He'd never wanted anything as much in his life. Throbbing and aching with desire, he drew his hips back, afraid he'd wake her. Afraid he'd lose control. Afraid he'd take her like a stallion at stud, all the while telling himself that one more time didn't matter.

Leave, he told himself. *Leave before it's too late.*

He couldn't though. He had to have one last touch, one last taste.

Drunk on desire and the intoxicating fragrance of gardenia, he bent over her and traced the tender curve of her mouth, bent closer and kissed her lightly. Once. Twice.

Oh, God, it wasn't enough. He was going crazy.

With supreme effort Matt eased back from her and tried to untangle his arms and legs without waking her. Sweat poured down his face though in summer his mother kept the thermostat low enough to freeze water.

Finally he got his legs and the lower part of his body free, which was a mixed blessing. Should she suddenly wake up, she'd have no immediate cause for alarm. But, Lord, he felt like a man climbing Everest denied the summit.

He was quietly trying to extricate his arm when Sandi rolled into him. They both went as still as deer facing the hunter.

"Matt?" she murmured, sleepy, cuddly, sexy.

"I didn't mean to fall asleep in the bed," he said.

He couldn't move. Her sweet body was curved into him, all her parts a perfect fit, and he couldn't have moved if elephants were stampeding the bedroom.

"I didn't want to wake you," she said, still not moving.

"That's okay. I was just going to the chair."

"No, please. Stay."

How could he refuse? He was holding heaven.

"I don't mean that the way it sounded," she said. "It's just that I want us to part good friends."

How good did she mean? His one-track mind took that tidbit and ran with it, and his body followed embarrassing suit.

Sandi didn't notice, which would be insulting if he hadn't rationalized that she was only *pretending*.

"We'll part friends," he said. "I'll just ease over to the chair now."

"Wait. I know I've made it hard for you...."

Amen. Any harder and he would explode.

"That's okay," he said, still hanging on, still hoping. For what, he didn't know. He was in no mood for soul-searching.

"And I know you don't...like me, and who could blame you after all the trouble I've caused."

"You didn't cause trouble, Sandi. Put that idea out of your head."

He felt like a soldier who had been holding himself at erect attention for two days. He ached in every muscle of his body. Even in his bones.

The longer he stayed in this bed with her, the greater his chances of not being able to leave. He pulled back but she caught his arm.

"No, please. I know I should have slept in the chair, but I thought, we're both adults, so neither of us should be deprived of a good night's sleep."

"That's what you thought?"

"Yes." Her pink tongue flicked across her full bottom lip, and once more he came undone. "But I thought something else, too."

She sounded like a little girl lost, and tenderness flooded him. He brushed her hair back from her face, her beautiful face that was going to haunt him the rest of his days.

"What was that, Sandi?"

"I thought how good it would feel to sleep curled up in your arms, and since you were sleeping so soundly and I couldn't ask you, I did it." In the dark they stared at each other, suspended. Then her tongue came out again, wet, sensual, crazy-making. "I hope you don't mind."

"No, I don't mind."

"Good. I didn't want you to think I was being fresh or suggestive or anything."

"No, I didn't think that."

"Well, good." Electric, that's how the air felt. "I wonder since it's almost morning and we've already… you know…would you mind letting me sleep like this till morning?"

"In the bed?" *Brilliant, Counselor.*

"In your arms. It feels so good and since I know you don't love me and I don't love you, there's no reason why we shouldn't, is there?"

His blood was on fire. His skin was burning. His heart. "No, no reason at all."

"Oh, good, then." She snuggled into him.

And God, the way she felt made him want to throw everything he had out the window, including his law practice, and run off somewhere with her. Vanish. The rest of the world be hanged.

"All right," he said.

And it was no great sacrifice at all to fold her in his arms, press his face against her hair and hold her, simply hold her.

* * *

For the first time since her father had died, Sandi woke up feeling loved. And all because she was sleeping in Matt's arms.

With the morning sun pinking the windows and casting a rosy glow over the covers, she studied him. He was very handsome in sleep, approachable and even vulnerable.

She knew she had been selfish to ask what she had of him, and yet she didn't regret it. When she left O'Banyon Manor this time she'd know they had been friends, at least in the end.

That was important to her. There was too much unkindness in the world, too much strife. She didn't want to add to that.

Of course, all her motives weren't noble. There was the simple fact that she loved him. Would always love him.

And now she had a really beautiful memory she could cherish the rest of her life. A kind and tender night that felt like love.

She eased out of bed without waking him, dressed quickly then sat down to write him a note. Afterward she propped it on the nightstand, then went downstairs to say goodbye to Lucy.

It was a cowardly thing to do, sneaking off like that, but she knew she couldn't bear to tell Matt goodbye in person. She couldn't pretend to be nothing more than a friend. She couldn't pretend the night had meant nothing to her. It had meant everything.

An hour down the road, she called C.J.

"I'm on my way home," she said.

"How did it go?"

"It was a pleasant weekend. Lucy's always fun."

"With Matt, I mean?"

"Nothing's changed, C.J. I'm coming home to get on with my life."

"Good girl. Clint and I have part-time carpenters lined up. We're starting the house tomorrow."

"I'll help. I'm not much of a carpenter, but I can fetch and carry. I need to be busy."

"I know, Sandi, you'll be okay."

"I wish I knew that."

Matt woke up to find his bed empty. "Sandi," he called, thinking she was in the bathroom. When she didn't answer, he called her again.

No answer. He glanced around the room. Her suitcase was gone and a note was on the bedside table. She had written:

Dear Matt,

You were sleeping so soundly I didn't want to wake you. Please don't think I'm trying to sneak off without saying goodbye: this note is my goodbye.

He stopped breathing, his heart stopped beating. He was a dead man holding a Dear John letter.

I want you to know that you are the best thing that ever happened to me. Not only did you bring me fully into womanhood—please know I have no regrets about that, only good memories—but you've made me see myself in a new light. In many ways I've been a child, and I've decided to do something about that. Thanks to you, I'm changing. And in positive ways, I hope.

Please know that whatever happens I will always cherish the time I spent at O'Banyon Manor and I will always hold you in tender regard.

She'd signed the note simply *Sandi.*

Stunned, he sat on the bed calling himself every kind of fool. Sometime in the wee hours of the morning while he watched Sandi sleep, he'd come to the startling revelation that he didn't want to lose her. Ever.

He'd decided to wait until morning to tell her of his epiphany, then he imagined the two of them making slow, sweet love together, for *real* this time, then going down to breakfast where they would plan the future.

Nothing permanent and earthshaking, just something sensible so they could get to know each other without the distractions of his mother's histrionics and their own ill-fated playacting.

Now she was gone. Suitcase and all.

Matt roared out of bed, jerked on his clothes and went in search of Lucy.

She was in the library standing in front of an easel. "Hello, Matt."

When she turned around he saw the portrait Sandi had done, Lucy sitting at the window, her expression so wistful it brought tears to his eyes.

"I know," Lucy said. "It's remarkable, isn't it?"

"Yes." He went closer so he could see the brush strokes, the colors, the wealth of detail that made his mother come to life on canvas.

"I've never had a better one. They always have me grinning or looking sophisticated or, heaven forbid, scholarly."

"Sandi sees with her heart," he said.

His mother gave him a quizzical look. And no wonder. He'd never said such a fanciful thing. He was more at home with facts and motives and the fight for justice, if such a thing existed.

"Yes, she does." Lucy stared at the portrait a while longer, then crumpled onto the sofa and put her face in her hands.

Alarmed, Matt squatted beside her with his hand on her shoulder. "Are you all right?"

"Oh, Matt. I've done you a grave injustice."

Lucy looked small and vulnerable, as fragile as a fine china teacup. Matt wanted to go back in time and hit his father.

"Mother, don't."

"Yes. It's time for the truth. Past time."

"You don't have to say anything, Mother. I know you know."

"How long?"

"Aunt Kitty told me while you were *dying*."

Lucy smiled, just as he'd intended, then she caught his hand and pulled him down beside her.

"That's not soon enough. I should have told you years ago that I knew Henry was cheating on me. I should never have let you carry the burden all by yourself.''

''It's all in the past now.''

''I don't think so. It still haunts you…and Ben. All those wasted years. All I had to do was admit the truth, then you wouldn't have grown up with your father's nasty secret eating you alive, and Ben and I could have had the life together that we deserve.''

''It's not too late for you and Ben. He loves you, Mother.''

''He told you that?''

''Yes. He's been waiting for you to face reality.''

''Well, I'm facing it now, and I *hate* what I see. You've lost Sandi because of me.''

''No, I let her go because of myself. But if I have anything to say about it, I haven't lost her.''

''I do hope not. Call me a hopeless romantic, but the minute I saw you two together at Ellie's wedding, I knew you were meant for each other.''

He put his arm around his mother and Lucy leaned her head on his shoulder, then they sat in silence studying the portrait. Sandi painted honest and true, seeing past the facade to the center of the soul.

Lucy's secret had taken its toll, and Sandi had captured it in her face. But she'd captured hope, too, and it was that element that both mother and son clung to as they sat side by side facing the future.

''I have to be going, Mother. I have to find Sandi, and this time I'm going to court her for real.''

He kissed her cheek, and when he left he noticed his mother was picking up the phone.

Matt didn't go directly to Sandi. He went home to Jackson to plan his campaign. This time he'd do the courtship right. When he'd finished, the siege of Vicksburg would look like a picnic in the park.

The next morning when he went to work he was whistling. Bob checked his watch, tapped the crystal to see if he'd read right, then said, "It's twenty after nine. Is the world coming to an end and I don't know about it yet?"

"No. All's well."

"Good, 'cause you've got a load of work on your desk."

Matt called his assistant and worked diligently till three, then buzzed Bob.

"Is that invitation for golf this afternoon still open?"

"You're going to play golf?"

"Thought I might give it a try."

Bob whistled. "Will wonders never cease?"

Sandi loved working outside getting sweaty and dirty. The kind of hard physical labor she did at the new house site gave her a pleasant ache she planned to soothe away with a good bubble bath and a glass of wine.

"Stay for supper," C.J. said and Clint echoed the invitation. He had already brought his grill out to their twenty-acre country place and set it up under the canopy of a hundred-year-old oak near the house site.

"Thanks, but I need to get home. I have some pictures to develop and I'm anxious to see if I've heard anything from the adoption agency.''

There was nothing from the agency, but there was a note on her door saying to call 555–6851, she had a special delivery.

She dialed the number. ''Hello, this is Sandi Wentworth. You have a package for me?''

''I guess you could call it that.'' The man laughed. ''If you're gonna be home, I'll bring it right over.''

Now, why would he laugh? Was it some kind of practical joke?

Sandi would have to postpone her bath. She wiped the smudges off her face and had just finished a tall glass of lemonade when her doorbell rang.

''Sandi Wentworth?'' She nodded. ''Sign here, please.''

''What am I signing for?''

''These.'' The man reached down and picked up a basket with two of the most beautiful golden retriever puppies Sandi had ever seen. She fell in love on the spot.

''But I didn't order any puppies.''

''No, ma'am.'' The deliveryman checked his invoice. ''Somebody named Matthew Coltrane sent 'em. You know him?''

''Well, yes, I do.'' Sandi felt a glow all the way to her bones.

''Reckon the feller must think right smart of you, then. Them puppies is purebred. Cost an arm and a leg.''

Sandi bent over the basket and two little pink tongues licked her face. "They're adorable."

"Yep. Them goldens is beautiful, all right. My cousin had one once. Growed up to be might' near a hunnerd pounds." He scratched his head. "I don't see how you gonna keep 'em in this apartment."

"It will be a while before they're grown. I'll figure that out when the time comes, I guess."

"I reckon you will. You look like a determined lady. Kinda remind me of Tallulah Bankhead, you know, sassy and pretty all at one time, if you don't mind my saying so."

"No, I don't mind." She gave him a big tip. "Thank you…" She read the name stitched in red on his shirt. "Fred."

"You're welcome, ma'am. You'll be needin' a vet. I got a cousin name of Sims Reeves over near Columbus can help you out."

"I'll keep that in mind."

"Oh, and this come, too." Fred pointed to another very large box. "I was 'bout to forget it."

"Thank you."

The talkative Fred finally left Sandi alone with her new puppies and the box, which turned out to be filled with puppy chow, two stainless-steel feeding dishes, two water bowls and two sleeping baskets with lamb's-wool pads.

At the bottom of the box, Sandi found a note.

Every girl starting over should have a pet. Two are better than one, don't you think? Matt

What did it all mean? Why was Matt sending her such an extravagant and thoughtful gift?

"Come on, children. We're going for a little ride."

She loaded her new puppies into the car and drove back to C.J. and Clint's.

"Good," Clint said when she got out of the car. "You changed your mind."

"Yes. And I brought guests."

Sandi unloaded her puppies and C.J. pounced. "What beautiful animals. Where did you get these?"

Sandi handed her the note. "I've always wanted a puppy. Remember how I begged Grandmother to let me have one? After she died I don't know why I didn't get one for myself."

"With our menagerie next door, you didn't need to." C.J. examined the two puppies from stem to stern. "They seem to be in good shape. We'll start their puppy shots tomorrow."

Sandi laughed. "Think what I'll save on vet bills."

"Yeah, just think."

"I don't know how long I'll be able to keep them in my apartment, though. Especially after I get the baby."

"Maybe Matt has other plans."

"You think so?"

C.J. hugged her. "Oh, honey, I hope so."

Chapter Twelve

Sandi didn't have any trouble making big decisions. She'd sold her house without a qualm, moved out of her grandmother's house without looking back and even filled out papers to adopt a baby with only a few butterflies in her stomach.

But when it came to matters of the heart, she remembered her awful track record and couldn't decide something as simple as picking up the phone and calling to say thank-you for the puppies.

Would a note be better? Would he think she was chasing him? Would she get so excited talking to him, she'd forget how she was going to make a new life on her own and say something to make him think she was weak and needy?

"I'm being a silly goose," she said, and both new

puppies licked her feet in happy agreement. ''Just pick up the phone and call. That's the ticket.''

Sandi picked up the phone and dialed. Sweat rolled down her face and she picked up a brochure on digital cameras to fan herself. When she heard the phone pick up, she got so excited she completely forgot what she'd been going to say.

''Hello,'' he said, but it turned out to be his recorded voice. After it clicked off, Sandi said, ''The puppies are wonderful, Matt. Thank you.''

She sat on the edge of the bed biting her lower lip and trying to think of something clever to say. Finally she just hung up.

''Oh, well. I'll write him a little note.''

Patsy and Pooh tugged at her shoestrings and she got down on the floor to play. They barked and pranced and wagged and Sandi laughed till she cried. It felt almost like having her own family.

Matt played Sandi's message four times, just to hear the sound of her voice.

''She likes them.''

He was pleased with himself. He hadn't spent years in a courtroom for nothing. It didn't take him long to sum up a person's character. Of course, Sandi had taken longer than most. She was a complex woman. Plus, he'd received confusing signals. Her bombshell body said one thing and her innocent eyes another.

Tomorrow he would send flowers, the next day candy and then he'd call her up and make a dinner date. Over a rare steak and some good wine he'd lay out his plan of action. It was a good sensible plan that would serve them both well.

Smiling, he picked up another of his mother's books, but not *Sinful*. It was probably a big gun, and he'd save it for last.

Patsy and Pooh gamboled around Sandi's feet, red roses delivered the day before scented the kitchen and a box of newly delivered chocolates lay unopened on the table. A letter from the adoption agency informing her that she'd been approved for motherhood was propped against the roses.

Still in her bathrobe and slippers, feeling slightly dazed, Sandi sat on a kitchen chair biting her bottom lip and waiting for C.J.

"Hurry, hurry, hurry," she said, and Patsy Cline barked her waiting's-a-lonesome-thing song.

The door banged open and C.J. bustled in. "Sorry it took so long, but I had to run by Bricks and Mortar, Etc. to check on toilet fixtures, then I stopped by Clint's office and left a sandwich for his supper along with strict instructions to eat it. He's so excited about owning his own newspaper that if I didn't remind him, he never would eat."

Usually Sandi wanted to hear all C.J.'s news, but today she had more pressing matters on her mind.

"Did you get it?"

"I got it." C.J. plopped an early-pregnancy testing kit on the table. "Thank goodness you called me instead of going yourself. You're in no condition to drive."

C.J. was right. Sandi was so nervous and excited and scared, she couldn't even open the box, let alone operate a car.

"Here, let me." C.J. ripped it open, scanned the instructions and then had to repeat them to Sandi twice before she understood.

"I'll be right back," Sandi said.

She thought she knew what the results would be even before she took the test. Since she'd left O'Banyon Manor the first time, she'd been so busy she hadn't noticed the missed periods.

When she woke up this morning feeling nauseated, she'd stayed in bed all day thinking she was coming down with a virus. By evening she was ravenous and feeling strong as a plow horse. While she ate everything in the kitchen except the sink, she'd noticed the heaviness in her breasts and she'd started counting backward.

Then she'd called C.J.

"Well?" C.J. asked when Sandi emerged from the bathroom.

Sandi ripped open the box of candy Matt had sent. "We need chocolate, and lots of it."

"You're pregnant?"

"Yes." All of a sudden it hit Sandi. At long last she was going to have the thing she most wanted in the world—a family of her own. Not one child, but two. And two dogs to make the picture complete. "Yes! Oh, C.J., isn't it wonderful?"

She caught C.J.'s hands and the two of them twirled

around the kitchen until Patsy was in such a barking frenzy that Pooh hid under a chair.

Sandi and C.J. collapsed into a couple of chairs then reached for chocolate.

"So, how are you going to handle telling Matt?"

"I don't know. I don't even know when I'll see him, or *if* I will."

"He's sent gifts every day. I think that's a pretty clear sign he wants to see you."

"Seeing me and marrying me are two vastly different propositions. I don't want him to feel trapped. I couldn't bear it if I thought he married me only because of the baby."

"I understand. I'd feel exactly the same way. With me it's love or nothing at all."

"That's exactly how I feel." Sandi dug into the chocolate. "This is the best I've ever tasted."

"They say everything tastes great when you're pregnant."

"I guess I'll get as big as a barn." Sandi giggled. "I can't wait."

"If you get too big to move, Clint and I will fetch and carry."

"I'll want the two of you to be godparents. For both my children."

"If you hadn't said it, I was going to horn in and insist."

Laughing, the two old friends ate chocolate until half the box was gone, then Sandi had a sobering thought.

"This little apartment won't possibly be big enough for two big dogs and two children. I'll have to find a house."

"Too bad you just sold yours."

"No. I don't regret that. It was a cold house filled with bad memories. I want something filled with light and warmth…and an antique four-poster bed."

"An antique four-poster bed?"

Sandi flushed. "Like the one in O'Banyon Manor. I want to give birth in a bed like that."

"I'll help you find one. I have another couple of weeks before I'm back in school. We'll shop tomorrow."

"Oh, gosh, I'll have to get baby clothes and a crib and…" Suddenly Sandi felt overwhelmed. "C.J., how am I going to do this all by myself?"

"You're not. I'm going to help you. Clint, too."

Though Sandi had already told her the details, including that her pregnancy didn't negate the adoption, C.J. picked up the letter from the agency and read it. The little girl Sandi would bring back from China was nearly two years old. She would be dealing with a language barrier, but at least she wouldn't be dealing with two small babies.

"It will be another two months before you go to China. You can still travel safely, and that gives us plenty of time to get ready for your little girl."

Sandi caught her hand. "What would I do without you?"

"You don't ever have to find out."

* * *

Matt checked his watch. He'd timed his arrival exactly right. He would be at Sandi's apartment and they'd have an hour to talk before dinner.

He was proud of himself. His plan was working out exactly according to schedule. He'd called a week ago, the day after she'd received the chocolate, and she'd said, "Yes, I'll be happy to have dinner with you."

Just like that. The reserve in her had surprised him a little, especially after he'd softened her up with gifts, but then, what had he expected? His invitation was a complete turnaround from his earlier stance.

He parked his car and went up her sidewalk whistling and bearing a corsage of gardenias, the fragrance so redolent of Sandi herself that he was having a hard time not acting like a sixteen-year-old schoolboy.

He punched the doorbell and suddenly there she was, glorious and radiant.

"You take my breath away," he said, then could have kicked himself.

Where was all the restraint he meant to use? The control? At the rate he was going he'd have her in the bed within the next ten minutes.

"Hello, Matt. Won't you come in?"

She'd turned off all the lights, lit candles, spritzed her exotic fragrance around the room. Make that five minutes if he didn't get hold of himself.

Suddenly two golden fur balls barreled into the room and launched themselves at his legs.

"I see the puppies are thriving."

Sandi scooped them both up and cuddled them close. "Aren't they adorable?"

It was on the tip of his tongue to say, *All three of you are,* but he caught himself just in time.

"Yes," he said, then took a seat across the room. No sense playing with fire. But even the small distance didn't lessen her impact.

God, she was the most stunning woman he'd ever seen. She absolutely glowed.

"You're looking good," he said. "Starkville agrees with you."

"Thank you."

Why did that make her blush? She was acting downright shy around him. Was he that intimidating?

As eager as he was to present his plan, he didn't want to plunge right in while she seemed so ill at ease.

"Sandi, we have a lot to talk about, but first I want to make sure you're completely comfortable with me. If there's anything you want to tell me, please go right ahead."

"What would I want to tell you?"

"To go to hell."

She laughed. "Oh, no. I would never tell you that."

"Okay. That's a good start."

"A good start for what, Matt?"

"An extension of our friendship."

She leaned her cheek into one of the puppies, and his heart grew two sizes. God, how could such an artless pose completely undo him? His plan flew out the window and he forgot what he'd been going to say.

"Of course I'm your friend," she said. "I hope we can always be friends."

"Good."

"Great."

He stared at her with such naked longing he wondered she didn't call bodyguards. Quickly he rethought his plan. Maybe three years was too long for a courtship. Maybe he could cut that down to two. Or one.

Matt took a deep breath. "I've been doing a lot of thinking since I saw you last." Okay. That was better. His libido was quieting down a little and his brain cells were beginning to kick back in. "I'd like us to spend more time together, get to know each other better."

"And?"

"And what?"

"Where is this leading, Matt?"

"To a courtship, I hope. You're a kind and wonderful woman, Sandi. The most remarkable I've ever met."

Visions of her in his bed sidetracked him, and he cleared his throat. Twice. God, how could he be so nervous? He was a trial lawyer, for Pete's sake. He'd faced hostile juries and enraged witnesses without blinking an eye. And now in the face of one soft and appealing woman, he didn't know his left foot from his right.

Maybe he should have read *Sinful.*

"Thank you" was all she said. Was that good or bad? Then, "Can I get you something to drink? Tea? Wine?"

"Wine, please."

She left in a swirl of swingy skirts and a cloud of heady scent that rendered him weak-kneed. He played with the puppies while she was gone and thought he'd regained his composure till she handed him the wine.

Up close she rendered him speechless. He wanted to touch her, to run his tongue over her dewy skin, down into that enticing cleavage. No, more than that. He wanted to take those intoxicating breasts deep into his mouth and suckle till they were both mindless with pleasure.

He took the wine with a polite thank-you, but he didn't breathe again till she was across the room and safely out of reach.

Slow down, old man, he told himself. The last thing he needed was a repeat of events at O'Banyon Manor. The last thing he needed was to fall into bed without thought of the consequences.

"This is good wine," he said. He noticed that she was drinking a large glass of milk. "You're not drinking?"

"No. I don't have much head for wine, if you recall."

"I do." *Vividly.*

Actually that's how it had all started, him putting her to bed. God, if he didn't get the bedroom off his mind…

"So do I," she said, beautifully flushed and looking more luscious than he'd ever seen. "How do you think people fall in love, Matt?"

"If you're asking do I believe in the fairy-tale romance my mother writes, my answer is no."

"Oh…"

"Not that I don't believe in love, Sandi. I think it

might be possible to grow to love a person if you spend a sufficient amount of time getting to know them really well.''

"How much time?"

"Two or three years." Her crestfallen look pierced his heart. "Maybe one."

"I think people who are meant for each other can fall in love at first sight. Maybe it's pheromones or something, I don't know. Pascal once said, 'The heart has its reasons of which reason knows nothing.' I really believe that, Matt.''

"It's romantic, I'll grant you that."

"What's wrong with romance?"

"What's wrong with careful planning and judicious decision making?''

"Nothing, really. It's just that the excitement of the unknown and the unexpected is such fun."

"You should be standing where I am when the excitement wears off. Divorce is not pretty, Sandi.''

She didn't say anything. Just gave him this *look*. God, how had he gotten off onto divorce? If there was a less romantic topic, he didn't know what it would be.

This conversation was not turning out at all the way he'd planned. Here he was offering her a reasonable courtship where, if there were no guarantees, at least they'd have a good shot at developing a bond that would last. And what did she do? Talk about romance and pheromones and excitement.

He'd forgotten just how unreasonable she was. Maybe three years would be better, after all.

She stood up and smoothed down her skirt. The gesture was artless, feminine and absolutely enchanting. How could that be? There wasn't a single thing reasonable about such a reaction.

"Can I get you more wine?"

"No. We should leave now if we're going to make our reservation on time. I hope you like steak."

"I love it." She smiled. "And I'm starving."

So was he. For Sandi Wentworth.

Matt felt vindicated. *See.* If he'd rushed things and let his passion get the upper hand he might not have learned whether she liked beef. It was a small thing, but success often depended on knowing the small details.

Sandi ordered a sixteen-ounce rib eye and ate the whole thing. Then she chose Mississippi black-bottom pie for dessert.

Matt watched her, amused, and she said, "Who can resist chocolate?"

"I'll have to keep that in mind."

Funny how she could hang her hope on such a small remark. Chocolate plus Matt equals fun under the covers, which leads to love and marriage.

She'd been doing that kind of wishful thinking all evening, ever since he'd walked in the door. Oh, he was delicious and she had a hard time keeping her hands off him.

But she must. She'd made up her mind not to do anything that would create an artificial closeness that wouldn't last. She knew Matt too well. If she seduced him tonight, he'd crawl into his cave, mull it over and decide he'd made some huge mistake that required an apology or even a complete withdrawal from her life.

And she certainly couldn't tell him about her pregnancy. She didn't want nobility from Matt. She wanted love. All or nothing at all, that was the way it had to be.

It only seemed fair, though, to tell him about her Chinese daughter. At least that way she'd know if he liked children. She'd tell him over chocolate.

When the waitress brought her pie, Sandi fortified herself with a bite or two then put down her fork and told him, "I'm going to adopt a little Chinese girl."

"You're *what?*"

Oh, dear. That was certainly not the reaction she'd wanted.

"I applied some time ago. I've been approved and I'll be leaving for China in the next couple of months to pick her up."

When he finally said, "Congratulations," she couldn't read between the lines at all. And no wonder. After all, he was a successful trial lawyer, trained to hide behind a mask of professionalism.

"Don't you like children?"

"We've had this conversation before."

She flushed, remembering how she'd awakened in his bed after a night of making love. She vividly remembered that. But what had they said about babies? She vaguely recalled prattling on about wanting a big family. Didn't she always? But what had he said?

She took a calming bit of chocolate before saying, "Refresh my memory."

"The conversation about children is premature, that's what I said."

"Well, of course, it's not so premature now, considering. Is it?"

"No, it isn't. I'm very happy for you, Sandi, and I hope I can get to know your little girl as well as you."

Now what? She'd asked for the moon again and received a pat on the head. Lord, was she ever going to quit wishing for things she couldn't have.

She picked up her fork and discovered there was no more pie. She'd have to muddle through without chocolate, that was all.

"Sandi?"

"Yes?" She gave him a bright, brave smile.

"Are you all right?"

"Yes," she told him, then suddenly she wasn't. She felt turned inside out. "Excuse me."

In the bathroom she grabbed a wad of paper towels, turned on the tap, held them under the water then swabbed her pale face with one hand while she clung to the sink with the other. God, she was going to faint. Wouldn't that be awful?

Somebody would find her in here passed out and then somebody would tell Matt and he'd ask her why and she'd probably tell the truth. Maybe that's what she ought to do anyhow. Tell him she was carrying his baby and simply put an end to all this suspense.

But, oh, she didn't want him to feel financially responsible for her *unforeseen developments*. Wasn't that what he'd once said? She didn't need financial help. She needed love.

Taking a deep breath, she straightened her shoulders and marched back to the table.

"Will you please take me home?" she said.

"Certainly. Are you okay?"

"I'm great."

"You're sure?"

"Absolutely."

The silence between them grew enormous, and he turned on the radio, some dreadful rap that gave her a headache.

"Do you like that kind of music?" she said.

"What kind?"

"Rap."

"Can't stand it." He switched stations and found one playing Pachelbel's *Canon*. "Is that better?"

"Much."

For a while there were no sounds in the car except the soothing magic of Pachelbel and the swish of tires on pavement.

"What are you going to name your little girl?"

"I don't know. Why?"

"I was just wondering."

Sandi wadded her hands in her lap to keep from reaching over and touching him. She wasn't about to build a whole new fantasy on something that small.

But when Matt parked the car and walked her to the door then stood there looking expectant and hopeful and not at all sure of himself, Sandi stood on tiptoe and kissed him lightly on the lips.

"Good night, Matt. Thanks for dinner."

"Good night, Sandi."

She didn't invite him in. She didn't have the kind of moral courage it took to offer him a cup of coffee then send him on his way. Oh, no. In spite of his cool logic and safe plans, she'd have offered him everything.

Inside she leaned against the door and whispered, "Goodbye, Matt, my love."

Matt stood on Sandi's stoop like a man shell-shocked. That she'd escaped being ravaged on her doorstep was a testament to his willpower.

Feeling like a man made of iron, he got in his car and sat there with the engine idling.

In spite of the fact that she loved the puppies and had enjoyed dinner, he had the uneasy feeling that something was amiss. He couldn't say that the evening hadn't gone well. But there was an undercurrent that had tugged at him all night.

He was in no condition to solve the problem now. Funny, how Sandi always threw him off kilter.

He would sleep on it, that's what. Give her time to mull over his proposition, then call her next week and suggest the ballet.

The International Ballet competition was going on in Jackson. Next Friday they were performing *A Midsummer Night's Dream*, which seemed to Matt altogether appropriate for his recent state of mind. That piece was romantic, too.

His plan was moving along right on schedule.

Chapter Thirteen

"I really like this bed," C.J. said.

"No," Sandi said. "I don't think so."

"What's wrong with it? It's mahogany, it has four posts, it's in good condition."

"It's a perfectly lovely bed."

"And?"

"It's not quite right, that's all."

The bed in question was in Clyde's Antiques on the outskirts of Starkville.

"That's the fifteenth bed you've turned down. I don't know where else to look."

"We don't have to buy a bed today."

"You're right." C.J. laced her arm through Sandi's and led her to the car. "You're not even showing yet."

"I'm not?"

"Don't look so disappointed. You can start wearing that new maternity dress if you want to. I think you look cute in it."

"I can't wait." Sandi climbed into C.J.'s car. "Let's get ice cream before we go home."

"Better yet, let's have dinner, then ice cream. Clint will be working late tonight getting out the Sunday edition."

"Don't you usually take his Saturday-night dinner to the paper?"

Blushing, C.J. laughed. "I'll call and tell him I'm keeping supper hot at home."

While C.J. called her husband, Sandi pressed both hands over her abdomen. She was lucky and blessed. Then why was she also blue?

"Sandi?" C.J. had come back from making her call. She placed a hand over Sandi's. "I know why you didn't like any of the beds. They weren't at O'Banyon Manor."

"Is that so awful?"

"No, honey. It's not awful," C.J. said as they made their way to the car and got in. "It's perfectly normal." C.J. turned the key in the ignition and drove off toward their favorite fast-food place for fried chicken without having to discuss it. "But I do think you might have given him one more chance. You love ballet. It would have been a nice outing for you."

"No. It would have broken my heart."

She didn't have to explain. C.J. understood. How could she sit beside Matt in the midst of something so romantic, so beautiful, wanting everything when she knew she could have nothing?

No, it was best this way.

Didn't clean breaks heal faster?

The auditorium was hushed, the ballet extravagant and the music beautiful. Matt sat on one side of his mother, with Ben on the other. Holding Lucy's hand, Matt noticed.

Seeing those intertwined hands made his heart hurt. He didn't want his heart to hurt. He didn't want to remember how he'd called Sandi and said, "I have two tickets to the ballet in Jackson, will you come?"

Maybe if he'd softened her up first, things would have turned out differently. Maybe if he'd said, "I've been thinking about your little girl, and I think you'll be a wonderful mother," she might have said yes.

He might even have said, "I've been thinking what it would feel like to be her father," but that was rushing things. Getting the cart before the horse, as Bob was always saying, in spite of the fact that he knew it was a tired old cliché.

"Matt?"

Lucy had that motherly look in her eyes. "The ballet's over."

"I was just waiting for the crowd to clear out. No sense stepping on feet when you can walk down a perfectly clear aisle unhampered."

"I see."

Lucy rubbed Ben's leg while she talked. Matt could hardly bear to watch. Not that he disapproved. On the contrary, he couldn't have been more pleased that his mother was finally getting the chance at the happiness she deserved.

But seeing them touch made him feel lonesome. Desperately lonesome.

Matt didn't want to be desperate about anything or anyone. He was a man in charge, a man in control. He'd spent years stamping out messy emotions. Then why was this one so hard to ignore?

"Sandi would have loved this ballet," Lucy said.

"Yes. I think she would."

"You should have invited her."

"Hmm" was all he said. In the face of Lucy's glowing romantic success, he wasn't about to admit his own failure.

Besides, he hadn't failed. He'd merely had a setback, that was all. He'd think of a brilliant comeback ploy.

Ben leaned around Lucy and said, "I guess this is as good a time as any to talk. I've been bursting ever since Lucy and I got here."

"Go ahead," Matt said.

"I love your mother, always have and always will, and since you're the oldest, I'm asking you for her hand in marriage."

"Nothing would make me happier," Matt told him, which was an outright lie. Having Sandi would make him happier. Having her by his side in the auditorium, her sweet scent wafting over him, her soft hand on his knee.

"Matt?" His mother was giving him that look again.

Good grief, he was going to make a fool of himself in front of his future stepfather if he didn't regain some semblance of control.

"When is the wedding?" he asked.

"In another year or so," Lucy said, laughing. "We're going to live in sin a while first."

"Lucy wants time to plan a big shindig," Ben said, and Lucy leaned over and kissed him on the lips.

"The kind we should have had in the first place," she told him.

"I'm taking your mother to Paris next week. Sort of a honeymoon before the wedding."

Lucy kissed him again. "Darling, all our times together will be honeymoons."

Matt was happy for them, he really was. Then why did he feel so miserable?

"Sandi's mother lives in Paris, doesn't she?" Lucy said.

"I think so."

"Maybe Ben and I will look her up, stop by to say hello." Lucy got that determined look on her face like a woman set to meddle.

"I don't think that's a good idea, Mother."

"I don't know why not. I'd like to tell that woman a thing or two about what a wonderful daughter she has."

Ben chuckled. "I see I'm going to have my hands full."

"You can count on it, darling."

This time it was Ben who initiated the kissing. Matt figured this was going to be the longest evening of his life.

"According to the ultrasound, I'd put your due date as February eighth."

The doctor's name was Samuel Jacobs, and he'd come highly recommended by two of C.J.'s classmates who were going back to school after having their families.

"Does that sound about right to you, Mrs. Wentworth?"

A sail at sunset. Oranges, key lime pie and Matt. Sandi got tears in her eyes.

"Yes," she whispered.

The attending nurse handed her a tissue, then patted her arm.

"And it's Miss," Sandi said. No sense pretending. She was having this baby all by herself.

"Will anyone be attending the birth with you?" Dr. Jacobs asked, not unkindly.

"Yes. My best friend, C.J. Crystal Jean," she added so there would be no mistaken ideas of the absent father coming to the rescue at the last minute.

"You're the picture of health, I see no reason why you shouldn't deliver a fine, healthy baby."

Sandi gazed at the monitor, seeing the heartbeat of her unborn child. The only thing that would make the moment perfect would be having Matt to share the joy.

She put on her new maternity dress then went to

tell C.J. and Clint the news. Her baby was going to be a lively, artistic, off-the-wall Aquarian.

Matt waited until after dinner to call Sandi. He'd stopped by to pick up a real man's meal of steak in order to provide himself an edge when he made the call. He tried never to go into a courtroom hungry or tired. A full stomach and a contented frame of mind could make the difference in how he presented his case.

He even waited thirty minutes after his meal to give his food time to digest. He'd meant to wait an hour but finally he couldn't stand the suspense any longer.

He picked up the phone and dialed.

"Hello." She sounded breathless and excited, like a little girl at Christmas.

Matt took that as a good sign. "Sandi, how are you?"

No plunging full speed ahead this time. Make small talk, plant the seeds, prepare the way. That was the ticket.

"Great. How are you?"

"Good. Keeping busy."

His mind went blank. He stood there listening to the sound of Sandi's breathing and feeling foolish.

"How's Lucy?" she asked.

"She's very happy these days. She's in Paris with the man she loved before she met my father. Dr. Ben Appleton. They're going to get married."

"In Paris?"

"No, I expect the wedding to be at O'Banyon

Manor. Sometime next year. Or, knowing Mother, it could be longer. She loves ostentation and fanfare.''

Sandi's laugh delighted him. It made him think of a little girl in a tree swing on a summer's day, light-hearted and full of childlike joy.

Suddenly he realized that was one of the things that drew him to Sandi. She exuded the zest for life that had always eluded him.

''I'm so happy for her,'' Sandi said. ''Your mother's a terrific woman and deserves nothing but the best.''

''Thank you. I think she's getting it this time.''

They both went silent. Listening to the soft sound of her breathing, he pictured her sitting in her den with her puppies curled in her lap. Probably wearing jeans and a T-shirt, or maybe something artsy, a swingy skirt that showed off her shapely legs and a pretty white blouse cut low and sliding off one beautiful shoulder.

''Sandi, do you like blues?''

''Oh, it's my favorite kind of music. So soulful and true.''

''There's a blues festival and barbecue cook-off next weekend in Jackson, Tennessee. Friday and Saturday. Lots of blues greats will be there, including Blind Bobby Walker.''

''Oh, I *love* him. He's a fantastic bluesman, absolutely my favorite.''

Matt smiled. Things were looking up. He'd made a good choice.

''I'm going, and I'd like it very much if you would go with me, Sandi.''

"Matt, I can't. I'm sorry."

Can't or *won't?*

There was something in her voice that told him it was the latter.

"So am I."

He said goodbye quickly because he didn't trust himself to linger on the phone after she'd turned him down. He might have gone into his lawyerly mode, asked a lot of questions that would not have advanced his cause one iota. He might even have lost control entirely and said, "Look, I'm coming up there to find out what this is all about."

He made himself a stiff drink and put on a good James Cotton CD then settled down on his big lonely sofa.

So what was another defeat? He'd lost another battle, not the war.

In times like this his mother was fond of quoting Scarlett O'Hara. "Tomorrow is another day."

For the first time in his life, the statement made sense to Matt. He'd call Sandi again, but not tomorrow. Maybe she had personal problems that had nothing to do with him. He'd give her some time to work them out. Give her some time to miss him.

The way he was missing her. Like losing an arm. Or a heart.

It was a Saturday night, which a song on one of his new CDs described as the lonesomest night of the week, and Matt couldn't stand being apart from Sandi a moment longer.

"To hell with the plan," he said.

He threw a few things into a bag, grabbed his shaving kit and his new travel case of CDs then headed out to Starkville, never mind that it was eight o'clock in the evening and by the time he got there it would too late to drop by unannounced.

And he certainly didn't plan to call ahead. He knew exactly where that would get him. Nowhere.

Mindful of the habit of highway patrolmen to lurk around after dark, Matt obeyed the speed limit— mostly—and passed the time by whistling along to his CDs. He was happy to say that he could now whistle every single tune.

As he clipped off the miles, he came to the startling conclusion that he would take up needlepoint if it would win him a place in Sandi Wentworth's heart. She had turned him into a bona fide romantic.

He stopped at a gas station forty miles from Starkville and called a Holiday Inn to make reservations. He'd check in, then be fresh and rested when he went to see Sandi early the next morning.

By the time he got to the outskirts of the city, he knew he wasn't going to check into a hotel without first driving by her apartment. At least to see if she was home. She could be out of town at an art showing or on a photographic assignment.

Her apartment was dark, her car gone. Matt couldn't believe it. Where was luck when he needed it most?

On the other hand, her deserted place proved that he was right about judicious planning. It beat dumb luck every time.

Maybe she'd be back tomorrow. That's what he told himself, but as he was getting ready to back out of her driveway some instinct stopped him.

Sandi was nearby. He could feel her prickling along the back of his neck and making his heart race.

A good lawyer never ignores his instincts. Matt parked his car then walked around the back of the apartment building to see what he could see. The land-lords had spent a lot of money making the entrance to their building inviting, but they'd done practically nothing to the back. A few scruffy crepe myrtle trees grew in an uneven line along the back, their leaves burnt orange by late September's chill, and a couple of tenants had set lawn chairs on the four-by-four-foot slabs of concrete that passed as patios.

By counting, Matt guessed the two tenants to be Sandi and her friend, C.J., who had the apartment right next door. There were lights and music drifting from C.J.'s apartment, but Sandi's remained dark.

Matt still couldn't believe it. Her presence was so close he could almost smell her perfume.

He stood perfectly still, hoping that no one would see him lurking in the shadow of the trees and mistake him for a burglar. Five more minutes. That's how long he would give himself.

Time crept by and he was just about to leave, when a light came on in Sandi's apartment. Silhouetted through the shades, she looked like a madonna with her long hair, graceful neck and the simple clothes she wore. Slacks and some sort of large shirt, probably an artist's smock.

He imagined it white and so pristine it made her skin glow. He imagined little flecks of paint spattered on the sleeve and one or two on her cheek.

''She's home,'' he said. That's all he needed to know.

As he was turning to go, he saw Sandi's shirt slide down her shoulders. Riveted, he watched it descend. There were her breasts, lush and fuller than he remembered, the slender rib cage hardly bigger than the span of his hands, and then...

Matt lost his breath as Sandi placed her hands over her abdomen and began to massage.

''She's pregnant....''

Every cell in his body ached with the beauty of Sandi's hands caressing the womb that held his child. Wonder sliced him like a knife blade. He couldn't have moved if fifteen cops were coming toward him with shackles. *Wouldn't* have moved.

There was a tenderness in the way she touched herself, a reverence that brought tears to Matt's eyes. Her hair swung like a curtain as she reached for more massage cream. He pictured it in the soft lamplight, a golden nimbus around her glorious face.

With every fiber in his body he longed to be in that room with her, touching her tenderly, rubbing the cream over her body.

Now he understood everything. How hopeless she must have felt when he'd talked about a three-year courtship. How her pride would have kept her from telling him, especially after that asinine offer he'd made to provide financial support for any *unforeseen developments.*

God, how could he have been so arrogant? So blind?

The child in her womb was real, it was wonderful, it was his. How could he ever have believed that he would consider it otherwise?

Sandi stood with her head bowed and her hands cupping her ripened womb. He imagined her talking softly to their child, perhaps singing. And standing in the dark alone, he felt deprived, like a castaway without food or water or hope.

The wise words of John Donne came to him: No man is an island. And yet Matt had tried to make an island of himself. He'd dug a moat and pulled up the drawbridge then dared anybody to cross.

But Sandi had braved his defenses and toppled them. And in his hubris he'd cast her off the island.

Now he wanted her back. Wanted her with a desperation that tasted like brine.

And not just because of the child. He loved the woman at the window. With the perfect hindsight that has been the cause of countless broken hearts, Matt realized that he had loved Sandi from the moment he saw her hat sail into his mother's swimming pool.

Why else would she have had the power to turn his life upside down?

The awesome beauty of it all was that Matt wanted the glorious upheaval of love. He welcomed it the way a lonely, sweaty traveler welcomes a stiff ocean breeze and a beachful of people yelling, "Come join the party."

He stood in the shadows until long after Sandi's window went dark, stood there paralyzed with wonder.

Chapter Fourteen

Sandi was putting the finishing touches on a commissioned portrait when her doorbell rang. She put down her brush and wiped the sweat off her face. Lord, she must look a mess. Who could that be?

Probably C.J. She'd said she was going to drop by after her morning class, but maybe she'd decided to drop by before.

The doorbell pinged again and she called, "Coming." She had almost opened the door but decided there was no sense taking chances. Putting her eye to the peephole she identified her visitor.

It was Matt Coltrane, bigger than she remembered, more handsome, more virile, more powerful. Sandi put her hand over her mouth to choke back a sound.

What was she going to do? She couldn't let him see her like this. She couldn't let him know.

"Sandi. Are you in there?"

Had he heard her call? Probably. Matt Coltrane never missed a trick.

He pounded on the door. "Open up, Sandi. I know you're in there."

"Just a minute," she said. What on earth was she going to say to him? "I'm not dressed yet."

She raced to the bedroom and threw a robe over her capris and shirt. The bare feet were fine. They'd give credence to her lie.

She reached up and mussed up her hair, then went to face him.

"Why, Matt," she said. "What a surprise."

She didn't invite him in but stood halfway behind the door.

"I would have called except I knew you'd refuse to see me."

"I *do* have a lot of work, Matt. I have to finish a portrait today after I wake up." She gave a fake yawn, congratulating herself on that authentic touch.

"I see." Now, why the devil was he looking so amused? "Maybe we could have breakfast together then. I was thinking of a large feast with sausages and eggs and buttered grits, everything fried and greasy the way we do it down here in the South."

The thought of it all made her stomach roll in protest. She felt all the color drain from her face and actually had to catch the door frame to hold herself upright.

"No, thank you," she finally managed to say.

"We'll skip breakfast then and get right to the talking. May I come in?"

"I'm not dressed, as you can see..."

If Matthew Coltrane was anything, he was a gentleman. Surely he would not persist.

"Yes, Sandi, I can see." His eyes raked over her and the heat of his gaze warmed her all the way to her bones. "I see your capris beneath that robe and the paint smudges on your cheeks."

He smiled, which was not at all what she'd expected. It wasn't just a polite smile, either. It was the kind that made her want to sit on the front-porch swing, if she'd had a swing, and hum romantic songs from the thirties, those terrific old songs that talked about red sails in the sunset and the glory of love.

"Let me in, Sandi, please."

His voice was deep and tender, and his face was so close and so dear. How could she possibly refuse?

She swung open the door and Matt walked in and stood there studying her as if he might never stop.

Nervous, she swiped at her cheek. He caught her hand and kissed her palm, then gently wiped the smudge from her cheek with the tips of his fingers.

"It's there." He smiled down at her. "And it's excessively charming."

"Oh..."

Closing her eyes, she put both hands over her mouth. *Don't let this be a dream,* she prayed.

"I was up early, painting."

"I know."

"I didn't mean to lie to you. It's just that—"

"Sandi, it's okay."

"It is?"

"Yes."

She heaved a sigh of relief, then realized she wasn't out of trouble yet. Even with the robe, her condition was still obvious to the trained eye.

"Can I get you something to drink?" she said. Maybe she could hide her bulging belly behind a serving tray.

"No, thank you. Let's just sit down, shall we?"

"All right."

She didn't sit on the sofa because the cushions were worn soft, and with her added bulk she felt like a beached whale when she tried to get back up. Instead, she took the wing chair with wide arms that would help hide her pregnancy.

"You look wonderful, Sandi. How do you feel?"

Did he know? He couldn't possibly. C.J. would never betray her.

"I feel great," she said. "But then I always do. I'm just a naturally healthy woman."

He was studying her again in a fiercely tender way that unsettled her. She caught her lower lip between her teeth and he smiled.

"I've missed you," he said. "More than I could ever have imagined."

Her heart flew home to nestle next to his, and it was all she could do to keep her body from following suit.

I must keep a level head, she told herself. There was too much at stake to make a hasty and unwise decision.

''Thank you,'' was all she said.

She sounded prim and distant, not at all like her usual exuberant, greet-the-world-with-arms-wide-open self. How could she possibly maintain this aloof pose with Matt so close he took up all the air in the room, with memories so sweet they took up all the space in her brain? Thinking straight was impossible.

All she could see was him. All she could think about was the handsome squared-off set of his jaw, how scratchy it felt against her cheek in the early morning as they lay in his family's four-poster bed, and how wonderful. As if it were yesterday, she recalled the strength and beauty of his legs, the feel of them between her thighs, the power of them as they held him suspended over her.

The air was electric between them as they held each other in steady regard, not speaking, barely breathing. Suddenly Matt was on his feet, striding across the room, a gorgeous and powerful male animal stalking his mate.

Her breath caught high in her throat and she couldn't seem to get it loose. She was going to faint. Right there in his arms.

He knelt in front of her and captured her hands in a firm grip that said, I'm not letting you go. Ever.

''Sandi, I want to marry you. I've wanted it since I first saw you.''

''Oh, Matt...''

Yes, she thought. *This. This is what I want.*

''Please say yes, Sandi. Let me make a home for you, and for our child.''

She drew back as if she'd been slapped. "You knew?"

"Yes."

"How?"

"I came here last night to see if you were home, and when I didn't see your car I went around back. I saw you silhouetted against the window shade."

He was still kneeling in front of her, too close, too real, too important. He was stealing all her air, robbing her of her senses.

She made a sound, not really a word but the broken, wounded cry of a dove who's not certain her babies are safe in the nest. If only she could believe he loved her.

"You knew I was carrying your baby before you decided to propose."

"I won't lie to you. I don't know what my intentions were when I left Jackson in the middle of the night. All I knew then was that I had to see you, I had to be with you."

He kissed both her palms. "Then when I saw you caressing our child, I knew I loved you. I *knew*, Sandi. All the reason in the world could not replace the simple truth in my heart. I love you, Sandi."

"If only I could believe it's true," she said. "If only I could *know*."

"What can I say, what can I do to prove it to you?"

"I don't know." She pressed her hands protectively over her abdomen. "I just don't know."

She wasn't wise in the ways of love. She'd made three terrible mistakes. And was it any wonder? Her mother viewed her as an inconvenience and her grand-mother had treated her as a burden to bear.

"Sandi, I won't press you for an answer. But I won't give up either. I want you to understand that." He smiled. "I'm not called Bulldog Coltrane for nothing."

"Bulldog?"

"That's what my colleagues call me."

"I'll keep that in mind." She loved the nearness of him, the way having his hands on her made her feel. Protected. Cherished. "Matt, I have to tell you something."

"I'm listening."

"My pregnancy does not change my plans about adoption. I'll be leaving for China within the next month to pick up my daughter."

"I understand that."

"Do you? We're a package deal, Matt. One pregnant woman, a little girl who doesn't speak English, and two puppies who will grow into very big dogs. That's a lot for somebody to take on, even a bulldog."

"I'm capable of the challenge. Give me a chance to prove it to you, Sandi."

"I don't want to do something that either of us will regret."

"Do you have regrets about us?"

"None, do you?"

"No."

Sandi saw how it was possible to get lost in a man's eyes. She saw how it was possible to glimpse his heart, his soul, and gazing at him she saw nothing except sincerity and truth. But was it merely of the moment or would it last a lifetime?

Sighing, he lifted his hand to her cheek and closed her eyes. "I just can't think right now."

"That's all right. Take your time. I'm staying at the Holiday Inn until Monday, and you have my cell phone. You can call me anytime, and I'll certainly call you."

"Matt, thank you. You've been more than kind."

"There's something I'd like to do before I go."

If he said *kiss* her, she knew she was lost. There was no way she could kiss Matt Coltrane and then refuse him anything, even a marriage that might turn out to be the kind of emotionally crippling experience she'd been accustomed to all her life.

"What would you like?" she said.

"To feel our baby. May I?"

Her heart melted, and she thought she was going to cry. Instead, she unbelted her robe and he pushed it aside. Then with the tenderness of a big man fearful of breaking English china, he spread his palms over her abdomen. The heat of his hands warmed her and made her feel safe.

As if he knew his father's touch, her baby chose that moment to make his first fluttering movements.

"Matt, did you feel that?"

When he looked at her, he didn't try to hide his tears. "I felt our child," he whispered, then he bent down and kissed her swollen womb.

She put her hand on his head, holding him there,

loving him there. And it was a very long time before either of them could speak.

Sitting in the hotel room staring at the telephone, Matt learned that waiting is the hardest thing in the world to do. Patience had never come easy for him, and yet he knew that if he pushed Sandi, he'd lose her.

He knew how to wait for verdicts, but they were always based on the case he had presented. Matt had the sinking feeling that he hadn't presented Sandi a very convincing case.

Furthermore, when he argued before a court of law he always armed himself with all the facts. While he knew everything about Sandi's spirit, her heart and her soul, he knew very little about her background.

But he intended to find out. He searched the phone book till he found the right number, then picked up the phone and dialed.

"Hello," she said.

"C.J., this is Matt Coltrane. I need to talk to you."

"Yes, you do, Matt. Sandi told me what happened."

"How is she?"

"Confused."

"I love her, C.J., and not merely because of the baby. But I don't know how to convince her of that. I don't expect you to betray any confidences, but if you can tell me everything you know about her, it might give me some idea of how to reach her. Can you meet me somewhere?"

"How does six at the Bulldog Grill sound?"

"Great."

The phone in their small apartment rang at two o'clock in the afternoon. Ben was on the balcony enjoying a cup of cappuccino and a view of the Seine while Lucy luxuriated on the bed, feeling decadent and as satisfied as a cat turned loose in a cream factory.

She picked up the receiver and said, "Hello," and her son said, "Mother? Is that you?"

"Of course it's me. What's put you in such a chipper mood?"

"Love…and fatherhood."

"What?" she screamed, and Ben came running.

"What's the matter, darling?" he said, and she caught his hand to anchor herself. "Dreams do come true," she told him.

"What's that, Mother?"

"I was telling Ben that dreams do come true."

"Almost. If I can convince Sandi.

"What do you mean, convince Sandi? She's been in love with you since all those crazy shenanigans at O'Banyon Manor. Of *course* you can convince her."

"I'm going to need a little help."

"From me?"

"Yes. I need you to locate Sandi's mother and let me know how to get in touch with her."

Ben handed her a pad and she scribbled furiously while Matt told her the name.

"Do you think you can find her for me?"

"Of course."

"You'll let me know as soon as possible. I'd like to be married to the mother of my child before the baby comes."

"You don't know how happy it makes me that you've finally let yourself love Sandi. I feel like a woman washed clean of guilt."

"You love her, too, don't you, Mother?"

"We all *adore* her."

"Then I have another proposal for you."

By the time her son finished telling her his plans and they'd said goodbye, Lucy was bawling like a newborn calf.

Sandi was in the darkroom developing photos of a christening while the dogs snoozed in their doggie beds when her doorbell rang. She stripped off apron and gloves, tucked a stray strand of hair into her ponytail then opened the front door to a deliveryman from Overland Express.

"Miss Sandi Wentworth? Sign here, please."

"I didn't order anything."

Behind him the doors of the truck clanged open and two men climbed inside.

"Just tell me where you want us to put it, Miss Wentworth."

"Put what?"

"This."

He stepped aside and there in her driveway was the beautiful mahogany four-poster bed from O'Banyon Manor.

She ran down the steps to the bed of her dreams.

Laughing and crying, she walked all around it touching the four posts, the ornate footboard, the massive headboard.

"I see you like my gift."

"Matt." Her baby kicked her so hard she could feel her maternity smock move. "Oh, Matt."

She put her arms around him and buried her face in his neck, inhaling the clean soapy scent that always lingered on his skin even after lovemaking. How could she not touch him?

He held her while the deliverymen waited patiently in her driveway.

"Go ahead and set that up in the bedroom on the right," he told them.

Sandi stepped back and smoothed her shirt. "I can't possibly accept that."

"The bed is yours. It's not negotiable."

"But, Matt..."

"No strings attached, Sandi."

"I'm going to cry again. I've been so emotional lately."

He smiled. "Other than that, how are you? Is everything okay with you and the baby?"

"Your son and I are both a hundred percent."

"My son?" Sandi wished for her camera. She'd never seen such joy bloom on a man's face. "I'm having a son?"

"The doctor is ninety-five percent sure. The second ultrasound made the baby's gender pretty clear."

He pulled her close and buried his face in her hair. "Oh, Sandi." His arms trembled, and she thought,

How can a man do that unless he truly loves? "Thank you, Sandi," he whispered.

"You're more than welcome, Matt. Oh, where are my manners? Would you like to come in for a while?"

"Yes, I'd like that very much. There are some things I'd like to discuss with you."

She didn't want to talk in front of strangers, so when they got inside, she said, "I'll fix us something to drink. Coffee? Tea?"

"I'll have whatever you're having."

"Milk."

He smiled. "Milk is fine."

She left him sitting on the sofa, and when she reached the safety of the kitchen, she put her hand over her mouth so he wouldn't hear her crying. She was such a mess. Crying for joy over a bed that had been special to her since the moment she saw it.

Could such a gift really come with no strings attached? When she went back with the milk she'd try to be more observant and less emotional. She didn't want her entire future to be predicated on the gift of a bed.

The deliverymen were leaving as she came out of the kitchen, so Sandi detoured by her bedroom to look at the bed. It was so wonderful it made her heart hurt.

She tore herself away then joined Matt, but she didn't sit on the sofa beside him. She didn't dare, not because of her bulk but because of her undecided heart.

But even across the room she knew her heart wasn't safe. How could it be when Matt was looking at her as if she were spun gold and he could survive only in the glow of her reflection.

"Sandi, when I told you the bed comes without strings, I meant that. Of course, I hope to be part of the package."

"I don't have an answer for you yet, Matt. I'm sorry. I've been so busy I haven't had much time to think, really. I'll be leaving next week for China."

"You'll need a bigger place."

She sighed. "I know. We'll just have to make do till I can find one."

"No, you don't. I want you to live at O'Banyon Manor."

"Till the baby is born?"

"No, permanently. As my wife, I hope, but your staying there is not contingent on marrying me."

"You can't be serious. That's beyond generosity. That's amazing."

"I've done a lot of thinking lately, and I've decided I don't want to live the rest of my life in my present rat race. I'm planning to open a branch of the law firm in Shady Grove."

"Lucy will be so happy."

"She is. She's also ecstatic at the idea of you living at O'Banyon Manor. The entire east wing would be ours...or yours if that's the way you prefer. It even has its own kitchen. We would be perfectly self-sufficient there. You wouldn't even have to consort with Lucy and Aunt Kitty unless you wanted to."

"Oh, but I'd love to." She bit her bottom lip. "If I lived there."

Matt smiled. "You can take your new bed, and I've already arranged a nanny to help you."

"I haven't said I'd go."

"When you decide, give me a call and I'll arrange for movers. And you don't have to worry about moving in and being bothered by me. I've already found an apartment in Shady Grove that will do fine until you make up your mind that I love you."

He stood and strode toward her, then knelt and kissed both her hands. "My love for you is real, Sandi. It's not going to vanish and neither am I. But until you decide for yourself, I want to take care of you. Please let me."

"You know how to tempt a girl, don't you?"

"I hope so."

She closed her eyes and breathed, simply breathed. It felt like the first good breath she'd drawn since she found out she was pregnant. Matt being in the room somehow made everything possible. Even miracles.

After Matt left she loaded Pooh and Patsy into the car then drove into the country to find her best friend. C.J. and Clint were standing in the middle of their framed-up house holding hands and watching the sunset.

They both waved at her, and C.J. called, "We're in the den. Come join us."

Pooh and Patsy raced off to chase a squirrel while Sandi picked her way across the littered concrete floor.

"Here, you get the best chair." Clint held her arm and led her to a timber laid across concrete blocks. "Is that sturdy enough for you?"

"It's great, thanks."

"Good. I want to learn how to take care of mothers-to-be. C.J. and I are pregnant." His grin was as big as Texas.

Whooping with delight, Sandi grabbed C.J. and the two old friends danced a careful version of the jig they'd used for years to celebrate the milestones in their lives.

"I'll just mosey off and watch after the puppies while you two catch up on girl talk."

"Thanks, darling." C.J. kissed her husband, then sat on the timber beside Sandi.

"Matt gave me the bed. Pinch me, C.J. None of this seems real."

"It's real, kiddo. He really does love you, you know."

"You think so?"

"I'd almost guarantee it."

"I guess that's what I'm waiting for, a guarantee. Everything's so wonderful right now. Perfect, in fact. I keep waiting for the other shoe to drop."

They didn't talk for a while. In the distance Clint tossed small sticks for Pooh and Patsy to retrieve, and a sun as red as Don Juan roses painted the sky with colors Sandi dreamed about.

"Look at him out there. Isn't he wonderful?" C.J. said, then turned to her friend. "Sandi, even if I knew it would all fall apart tomorrow, I'd still take my chances. I'd rather have a few months with him than a guaranteed lifetime with a man I didn't truly love."

Chapter Fifteen

Sitting in the airport with a small tote bag packed full of little girl's clothes, size eighteen months, Sandi tried not to be nervous. The doctor had nixed C.J.'s plans to accompany her to China because she was in the first trimester of her pregnancy, and of course Clint needed to be with his wife.

Sandi dug into her purse and brought out a candy bar. If she didn't find relief from stress soon, she was going to be so big she wouldn't fit between the posts of her fabulous old bed. Sighing, she put the candy bar back into her purse.

"Be strong," she said. "Resist temptation."

"There's no reason to."

Matt stood there in the sunshine smiling down at her, and suddenly she knew the meaning of heaven.

PEGGY WEBB 235

"Matt, what on earth are you doing here?"

He slid into the seat beside her. "You didn't think I was going to let you go to China all by yourself, did you?"

"I'm perfectly capable of taking care of myself."

"I know you are, but did you think I was going to let you get a head start on me and worm your way into our daughter's affections before I ever got a chance to win her heart?"

"*Our* daughter? Did you say *our* daughter?"

"Yes, our daughter, Sandi."

She fumbled in her purse. Drat it. Where was a tissue when she needed it?

Matt pulled out a perfectly laundered, perfectly white handkerchief and she destroyed it with mascara and tears.

"I'm sorry," she sniffed. "I'm such a mess. You must think I'm hopeless."

"On the contrary. I think you're the most remarkable woman I've ever known." He took the handkerchief and wiped a smudge she'd missed. "There now, is that all better?"

"All better," she said, meant it. The simple fact was, being with Matt always made everything better for her. But could she trust it to always be so?

"They're calling our flight," she said.

"So they are. Give me your ticket, Sandi."

This time she didn't question. She was too grateful to have someone else in charge for a change.

"What was that all about?" she asked when he came back.

"I've upgraded us to first class. Pregnant women need more room to stretch their legs."

"How did you know?"

"The same way I know lots of things." He kissed the tip of her nose. "The same way I know you're going to marry me."

"I haven't said yes."

"I plan to work on that."

Sandi couldn't think about all the implications of what he'd said. Lately she tired easily, and she had to conserve all her energy, both physical and emotional, for the task ahead: getting her Chinese daughter.

In fact, she was so tired that she began to nod off as soon as their plane reached cruising altitude.

"Would you please bring a blanket and pillow," Matt told the flight attendant.

Instead of handing them to Sandi, he insisted on tucking her in.

"Thank you," she said. "You're really very sweet."

"That will do for starters."

She tingled in delicious ways and hoped he didn't notice. It was getting harder and harder to maintain a noncommittal stance with Matt. For one thing, he was doing everything possible to meet all her needs without asking a single thing in return. Not even a kiss.

For another, having him around to help secure her adopted daughter, plus make way for her unborn child, was such a relief, she was sorely tempted to say yes to him on that basis alone.

She leaned her head against the window and closed her eyes.

"Why don't you lean this way? My shoulder would be much more comfortable."

She started to say no, but the flight to China would be very long and she was extremely grateful for his company.

"Thank you," she said.

When she leaned into him and he put his arm around her, it felt exactly right.

He bent down and kissed the top of her head. "Just rest," he said. "We have a long journey ahead."

She sighed once, then gave herself over to sleep.

Holding her in his arms, Matt owned the universe. He would do anything for her, including protect her from his own impatient passion. Over the last few weeks he'd fought a mighty battle to keep from using sex to persuade her to be his wife.

Sandi's blood ran hot, and when you combined that with her loving heart, it made her vulnerable.

Matt considered himself an honorable man. He wanted Sandi to come to him out of love, not out of the heat of the moment. If that made him old-fashioned, so be it.

On the upside of all this restraint, he was constantly on fire with anticipation. Nothing is sweeter than love long denied. He'd read that somewhere. Probably in one of his mother's books.

He smiled thinking of Lucy. She and her sister Fox had done the job in Paris. They'd found Sandi's mother living not far from Ben and Lucy's apartment.

In another stroke of good luck, Meredith Wentworth

Perkins Santiago Garber Martin Levalier was between husbands. Or as she put it, "Honey, I can't get another man without a face-lift, and if I get another face-lift my ears will be on top of my head."

She wasn't what Matt had expected, especially after he was so blunt with her.

"Time is of the essence here, so I'll be perfectly frank," he'd said. "Your daughter is pregnant with my child, but she won't marry me because she expects every person in her life to abandon her. She actually thinks your leaving her was all her fault. She believes no one can love her because she's unlovable."

"My God, Sandi's beautiful, resourceful, independent. She didn't need me. I was an awful parent. I did her a service getting out of her life."

"That's not the way I see it."

Sandi shifted in her sleep and the blanket slid off her lap. Careful not to wake her, Matt picked it up and tucked it tenderly around her shoulders. Then, holding one arm around the woman he loved and one hand protectively over his baby, he prayed that everything would turn out the way it should.

They had rooms with connecting doors. "Just knock if you need me," Matt had said.

Sandi didn't want to need him, but nothing felt more isolated than being alone in a bed in a strange city half a world away from home where you didn't understand the language, the people and the culture. Sandi was exhausted. All day they'd had to depend on strangers to interpret for them and lead them through the maze they called a city.

Getting a Chinese girl wasn't as easy as presenting yourself and saying, ''I've come for my child.'' No. You had to bribe your way through a seemingly endless line of officious-looking people.

Thank God, Matt had been there to deal with that. She didn't know what she would have done without him.

Her feet felt like sausages. She rolled to her side trying to get comfortable. When that didn't work, she tried propping up on a pillow. It looked as if steamrollers had run over it. It wouldn't prop up an ant, let alone her burgeoning belly.

''What's the use?''

Throwing pride out the window and caution to the winds, she knocked on the connecting door. Matt opened it so quickly she wondered if he'd been standing on the other side listening to her toss and turn. She wouldn't be surprised.

''Hello,'' she said, suddenly shy. She hadn't thought to put on her robe, and she was still wearing the sheer gowns she loved. Not that she had anything to hide. And certainly not that she was enticing. Good grief, she looked like a pregnant hippo.

''Hello, yourself.''

He smiled, and she felt better already. ''I can't sleep.''

''Neither can I. Why don't we be awake together?''

God, she loved him, making it seem as if sleeping together had been his idea instead of hers.

"Okay," she said, and he took her hand and led her to his bed.

She thought about lying on her side of the bed, then giggled at the idea. It was a little late for primness.

"What's so funny?" he said.

"Nothing. I giggle a lot."

"It's a lovely sound."

"What a nice thing to say. You're really a very sweet man, Matt Coltrane."

"Better not pin any medals on me yet. Sweet is not what I'm feeling right now."

He was looking at her like a man starved, and she responded with her whole body. Good heavens, she hadn't known a pregnant woman could feel like a shameless vixen.

She scooted toward her side of the bed and plumped up her pillow.

"Yours is bigger," she said.

"I beg your pardon?"

She felt hot from head to toe. "Pillow. Your *pillow* is fluffier."

"I see."

Thank goodness he didn't laugh. She closed her eyes and covered a big yawn.

"Isn't it funny how you can sleep better when somebody else is in the bed," she said.

"*Astonishing* is the word I'd choose. I thought being alone was the ideal state until I met you."

"Hmm. You're so..."

She fell asleep in midsentence.

Matt propped himself on his elbow and watched her

sleep until he could hardly hold his eyes open. Then very carefully he wrapped his arms around her and pressed his face into her soft shoulder.

This, he thought. *This is the ideal state.*

Sandi dreamed she was in the middle of the ocean surrounded by sharks. Desperately she searched the horizon, but there was no one in sight, no one to come to her rescue. She would drown all alone, unless the sharks got her first.

She startled out of sleep, panicked, then felt the comforting presence of Matt's warm, solid body.

"Sandi?" His voice was sleepy, sexy, his arousal instant. "Are you okay?"

"Oh, Matt."

She'd never needed another human being as much in her life. The instant she pressed into him she changed from scared to excited. *Extremely* excited. Beyond control, actually.

Shifting so the fit would be right, she slid her hands between the sheets and guided him toward her hot, shameless body.

"Sandi?"

"Please…" she whispered, and suddenly there was heaven. Their joining was so beautiful, so right it made her cry.

"Am I hurting you?"

"No. Please, don't go." She pulled him back down and pressed his head against her breasts. "Just don't go, that's all."

"Never," he said, then took an engorged nipple and

began to suckle. He was so tender it broke her heart, so wonderful it thrilled her soul, so magical it transformed her body.

She was no longer awkward in her advancing pregnancy but the most desirable woman in the world. She was a geisha trained in the arts of pleasure, a sought-after courtesan renowned for her unbridled passion and inventive ways.

In the rich dark warmth of the room redolent of the exotic scents of sandalwood and ginger, Matt explored her like an archaeologist uncovering a lost city of gold.

He touched every part of her, exposing her nerve endings and excavating her emotions. As tidal waves of pleasure ripped through her, she knew what it felt like to be loved. Finally she knew.

Theirs was not merely a bonding of bodies, but a melding of souls. True love needed no words. It needed only this paradise.

She arched high to meet him, and he slid a pillow under her back to give him easier access to that deep, secret place that no man had ever touched. That no man would ever touch except Matthew Coltrane. The man she loved. The man she would love forever.

She woke up late in the morning, and Matt was fully dressed, sitting in a straight-backed chair watching her.

''Good morning, sleepyhead.''

He smiled, and it was the most beautiful sight in the world. She felt wonderful. She felt like Scarlett O'Hara after Rhett Butler finally stormed her chaste bedroom and gave her a night to remember.

Flushed, Sandi threw back the covers. "Good heavens, we're going to be late."

"No. I went down and took care of a few things while you were sleeping."

"Greased a few more palms?"

"Yes."

"I'm glad I didn't have to go through that. Thank you, Matt."

"You're more than welcome." That smile again. "For everything."

Oh, Lord, if he mentioned last night she was going to die. She couldn't think about that right now. Last night she'd thought she'd glimpsed forever, but in the cold light of day with a cacophony of foreign sounds outside her window and legal red tape a mile long between her and her adopted daughter, she couldn't see beyond the next moment.

"I left a note in case you woke up while I was gone. I'm glad you slept. You need the rest."

"I feel much better today." She blushed again. Lord, she felt like a bride. "I guess I'd better get dressed."

"Take your time. I'll go down and get us some food. That way, you don't have to leave the hotel until three o'clock unless you want to."

"Three o'clock?"

"That's when we see our daughter."

He slipped out of the room as quietly as a shadow while Sandi sat on the bed hugging her knees and loving him with all her heart. She stayed that way for a long time, reveling in the ripeness of her body and the richness of being loved.

She took a leisurely bath, then dressed and was combing her hair when she heard the knock.

"Matt?" Why was he knocking? Had he forgotten his key.

"No," a female voice said. "Not Matt."

Sandi stood riveted, her hand over her throat.

"Sandi." The knock again. "Aren't you going to let me in?"

Slowly she opened the door. "Mother?"

"Yes, Sandi. It's your mother, better late than never, I hope."

"But how? Why?"

"Matt found me and told me a few truths I needed to know, then paid for my ticket here. May I come in?"

Still stunned, Sandi led this almost-stranger into her bedroom then sat with her hands folded and her ankles crossed as if she were six years old, still waiting for her mother's approval.

"Sandi, I'm a frivolous woman who has lived a selfish life, but there has not been a moment in all these years that I didn't love you."

"You left me."

"You were always independent, just like your father. And I thought you'd be better off without me."

"How could you think that? You're my mother."

"I've always been self-centered and flighty. I thought Mama would do a better job raising you than I would."

They stared at each other a long time, mother and daughter finally in the same room. They might as well have been oceans apart.

"We'll never know, will we, Mother?"

"No. The past is over and done with, but we still have the future. I'd like to be a good grandmother, if you'll give me the chance."

Sandi could say no. She'd survived the crucial childhood and teenage years without her mother. She could certainly survive adulthood without her.

"All right. It's okay." Meredith stood up. "Be safe, Sandi. And please know that whatever else I did, I always loved you."

Drowning in a sea of emotions she couldn't begin to sort out, Sandi watched her mother walk toward the door. Suddenly one clear thought popped up, a life jacket on which she could float.

"I love you, Mother." Meredith started to cry, and Sandi embraced her then held on. "I want you to stay," she whispered.

Matt fell in love at first sight. The little girl had a cap of shining black hair, two bright button eyes and the smile of an angel. He and Meredith stood back while Sandi knelt beside her new daughter, Kim Yong Ling.

"Hello, Kim. I'm your new mother." Kim put her thumb in her mouth and stared. Sandi put one hand over the little girl's heart, then took her tiny hand and held it over her own. "I love you, and soon you will love me. I'm going to take you home to America and love you the rest of your life.''

The tiny thumb popped out and the rosebud mouth formed her first English word. ''Love,'' she said, and Sandi wrapped her close and buried her face in the soft dark hair.

They stayed that way for a long while, and finally the little girl's arms stole around Sandi's neck. Sandi turned around and beamed at Matt.

''She likes me.''

''Who wouldn't?'' he said.

Sandi picked her daughter up and brought her over to Meredith and Matt.

''Kim, this is your grandmother.'' Meredith stood there as if she didn't know what to do, which didn't surprise Matt. He was glad to have her there at all. Perhaps the rest would come in time.

Sandi took the child's hand and patted her mother's cheek, then suddenly she was standing in front of him and he felt as helpless as Meredith looked.

''This is your daddy.''

The baby's angel smile released him. He picked her up and hugged her like an old pro. She smelled like sunshine and scented bathwater, and he wanted to cry.

''You're going to love your daddy. He's the most wonderful man in the world.''

The way Sandi said it made Matt think it just might be true.

''Hi, little angel,'' he said.

''I thought we'd call her Kimberly Lucille, after your mother. Do you think she'll mind?''

"Mind? She'll call a press conference and brag to the whole world."

"Kimberly Lucille Coltrane," Sandi said. "That's what I told them to put on the adoption papers. I listed the father as Matthew Coltrane."

"And the mother?"

"Sandi Wentworth Coltrane," she said.

And suddenly there was paradise.

The four-poster mahogany bed was back in O'Banyon Manor, and Matt was stretched out on it waiting for his wife. He smiled when he heard her footsteps.

"Matt?"

"Why is it so dark in here?"

She reached for the switch and he said, "Don't turn on the lights. Come closer so I can look at you."

"At us, you mean. We're getting huge."

"I have something for you."

He threw aside the sheets and her eyes widened, then she began to smile.

"Kimmy Lu's sound asleep," she said.

"Good."

Feeling like the hero in an X-rated movie, he got off the bed and slowly removed his wife's gown. Then he handed her a wisp of lingerie no bigger than a sneeze.

"Put these on."

With her hands over her abdomen she giggled. "We'll look like a barrel."

"You'll look like the sexiest woman in the world."

She stepped into the naughty panties, and it was a while before he could pull himself together. At the rate he was going, he figured they'd have about seven children before they ever stopped for breath.

"Well?" She gave him a sassy, sexy smile. "How do I look?"

"Good enough to eat."

He reached behind him for the red ribbons, the feather boa and the apricot oil. Sandi's eyes flew to the bedside table. *Sinful* was still open to page 161.

"I see you've been doing some more research."

"Yes. Do you want me to tell you what I discovered?"

"Why don't you show me?"

"My pleasure, Mrs. Coltrane."

Matt lowered her to the bed where generations of his family had been conceived and born, where his own children would be conceived and born.

Then he tilted the bottle and oil pooled between her ripe breasts.

"Is this a long scene?" Sandi asked.

"A very long scene."

He took the ribbons and the feather boa, and after the moon shadows had moved completely off the bed, Sandi said, "Remind me to thank your mother."

"I already did." He lay down beside his wife and fitted her tenderly in his embrace.

"You make me feel loved," she whispered.

"I plan to see that you and all our children feel that way. Always."

Then he closed his eyes and fell into a deep, dreamless sleep in the bosom of his family.

*   *   *   *   *

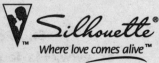

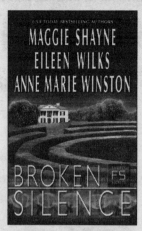

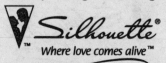

Coming in April 2003

baby and all

Three brand-new stories about the trials and triumphs of motherhood.

"Somebody Else's Baby"
by *USA TODAY* bestselling author Candace Camp

Widow Cassie Weeks had turned away from the world—until her
stepdaughter's baby turned up on her doorstep. This tiny new life—
and her gorgeous new neighbor—would teach Cassie she had
a lot more living…and loving to do….

"The Baby Bombshell" by Victoria Pade

Robin Maguire knew nothing about babies or romance.
But lucky for her, when she suddenly inherited an infant, the sexy single
father across the hall was more than happy to teach her about both.

"Lights, Camera…Baby!" by Myrna Mackenzie

When Eve Carpenter and her sexy boss were entrusted with caring for
their CEO's toddler, the formerly baby-wary executive found herself
wanting to be a real-life mother—and her boss's real-life wife.

Where love comes alive™

SPECIAL EDITION

#1537 THE RELUCTANT PRINCESS—Christine Rimmer
Viking Brides

Viking warrior Hauk FitzWyborn had orders from the king: bring back his long-lost daughter. Well, kindergarten teacher Elli Thorson wouldn't be *ordered* to do anything by anyone, handsome warrior or not. But Hauk intended to fulfill his duty and protect the headstrong princess, even if that meant ignoring their fierce attraction to each other....

#1538 FAITH, HOPE AND FAMILY—Gina Wilkins
The McClouds of Mississippi

When the safety of Deborah McCloud's family was threatened, Officer Dylan Smith was there to offer protection. But old wants and old hurts seemed to surface every time the one-time loves were together. Could their rekindled passion help them overcome their past and give them hope for a future—together?

#1539 MIDNIGHT CRAVINGS—Elizabeth Harbison

Chief of Police Dan Duvall was a small-town man with simple needs. So, why was it that city slicker Josephine Ross could stir passions in him he didn't know existed?

#1540 ALMOST PERFECT—Judy Duarte
Readers' Ring

A commitment-phobic ex-rodeo rider like Jake Meredith could *not* be the perfect man for a doctor, especially not an elegant Boston pediatrician like Maggie Templeton—not even when he was her best friend. But when Maggie's well-ordered life fell apart, could she resist Jake's offer to pick up the pieces...together?

#1541 THE UNEXPECTED WEDDING GUEST—Patricia McLinn

Max Trevetti could *not* be having these intense feelings for Suz Grant.... She was his sister's best friend! But Suz was no little girl anymore; their escalating passions seemed to prove that. Would Max and Suz turn away from their desire, or risk everything for love?

#1542 SUBSTITUTE DADDY—Kate Welsh

Brett Costain was just as faithless as his father...wasn't he? That's what he'd been told his whole life. But sweet, small-town girl Melissa Abell made him almost believe he could be husband material—and even a father to her baby—as long as he could convince *her* to be his wife!

SSECNM0403